A Pictish Tale:

BRYHERY GAP

Mark Youds

This First edition Paperback first published by Mark Youds 2008
© Mark Youds 2008

Text and Illustrations copyright © Mark Youds 2008

Mark Youds asserts the moral right to be identified as the author and artist of this work

ISBN: 978-0-9556865-1-1

Printed and bound in the United States of America by Lulu

Lulu website is: www.lulu.com

Bryhery Gap. AAAAAAAAAAAAAAAAAAAAAAAAAAAAAAAAAAAAAAAAAAAAAAAAAAAAAAAAAAAAAAAAAAA

PREFACE

In an Ancient land long ago; a nation of Picts lived on 'The Island' in the northern hemisphere. At the furthest point north and north-west of the boundaries of their land (Sunna), stood a huge glacial cap. The far western point of Sunna included the AnTara hill range of Ru. In the far south, stretching for some thirty-eight miles, was the Eyribol Ridge, a nineteen mile wide compressed bank of sandstone that held back the sea. 'The Island' itself actually extended an equal distance again both further south-east and north of Sunna. High mountain peaks stretched along the west and eastern horizons, from where it looked an inhospitable place, with a line of impenetrable cliffs.

Although Sunna accounted for only about one-quarter of the Island, its boundaries meant that the other three-quarters were split into three separate regions. To the west, lay the green land of Ru, which was divided in two by a fifty-seven mile wide ancient oak forest.

Along the eastern coastline of the Island, from Tyne-cave to the the far south-east of Belevedon, was an unnavigable fast-flowing sea-river – which separated the Island from a narrow stretch of numerous tiny islands known as Dogger.

The vulnerable expanse of the Eyribol Ridge was guarded by a much larger race of beings that kept a safe road open for their own kind. The Finns, who resided in Belevedon, had guarded the Eyribol Ridge longer than any Pict had been alive, and yet the Finns never seemed to age. Few Picts knew that they were inadvertently being protected by actual people, and even less knew of the existence of Finns.

Finns had long white hair and bright grey eyes that shone during the day and glowed in the night. The humans, who lived on the Dogger isles, thought that all Finns looked alike; which was not correct, due to the fact that a Finns age could be determined by the length of their eyebrows, nose and ears. (*If an ordinary Pict saw any of the Finnic folk, they thought they were the Urs* [dead spirits] *of a forgotten race. In truth, at least once every year, the Pict's true Urs did come to advise the tribe, during the 'Urinox'*).

The King of the Picts knew that the Finns would sometimes migrate from a bay they called Portowest. Where to, he didn't ask. Most Picts regarded themselves as guardians only of the land known as Sunna, 'The Lady of the Sun', an area lying within a circular boundary whose radius, of about one hundred and eighty miles, emanated from Manni's island. As such, they usually lived no more than six miles from the shores of the enormous landlocked lake that covered most of the central area of the Island.

On the eastern shore, the great lake would flood into a vast open natural vat, leaving it teeming with 'Kala' fish. This area was known as Ganjara, the 'Pool of Life.'

Picts were usually bald, had greyish skin and could be mistaken for moss-covered boulders. They did not eat red meat, and kept fowl only for their eggs and cows for their milk. Outwardly, the various tribes living in areas more abundant than others appeared to trade with one another. In fact they were actually sharing out produce in accordance with the size and needs of each tribe. Any overriding decisions were made by the King, from the Taezali tribe – who were the only nomadic tribe that trod a path in accordance with the turning of the Moon-Sun cycle.

At different times of the year they visited specific sites in order to stay attuned to, and work with, the nature spirits. These spirits were not worshipped, invoked or appeased, but were treated as allies.

There was also an autonomous state lying across the borders of Sunna and Belevedon. In the mountains, east of Eyribol, lived the Gridolers; distant cousins of the Picts. At just over four feet in height, a good foot taller than a Pict, they had a similar stocky build and bald heads, but with dark brown skin rather than Pictish grey.

To look into a Gridolers eyes, which are completely black, is like looking at a starlit night being reflected off a lake as smooth as glass. The whole eyeball was a dark pupil, with a single circular eyelid that would involuntarily contract according to the amount of light available.

Gridolers also lived south of Sunna, in what is the far west of Belevedon. They had tunnels running from the mountains, under the Tajem trees and out into Belevedon.

The Tajem provided protection for the Picts, because almost the whole of Sunna was surrounded by a nineteen mile deep forest of close-knit Tajem trees. The trees of the outer perimeter were so closely packed together that it was impossible to pass between the trunks without brushing against the trees. Tajem bark contained a substance that could kill all, except Picts. Anyone breaking their skin against one of the trees would be dead within an hour!

Chapter 1: **PICTLAND**

Pan was lying on the side of the lake with his muscular, goat-like, legs unceremoniously stretched out into the water. A dragonfly, that had been skimming across the lake's surface, came and perched upon his nose before walking down his beard; easing Pan gently from his slumber. He picked it up and focused on its delicate red, turquoise and green shimmering wings. 'Such ancient beauty,' he thought to himself.

Pan always welcomed these lovely summer days of sunshine, butterflies and bees.

The dragonfly flew off.

Yawning, he rested his head back down on a pillow of reeds and watched the Water-Lilie-spirits dance around him. 'What a life,' he thought. 'It has been so peaceful for so long that I really could get quite used to this.' He smiled to himself. 'Yes. Why not. I shall extend the summer again for a few weeks this time.' He stopped to consider his next move. 'And then .... soon.' His eyelids narrowed, almost menacingly, as he gazed northwards. 'Soon I shall remove the final remnants of this ice-age.' Humming softly to himself, his eyelids began to droop again. The humming turned to snoring.

Pan made such a loud grunt, that he woke up with a jolt; reminding himself that he hadn't quite finished his musings yet. 'I will have to make the winter a bit wetter, just to keep the balance.' If it hadn't have been for the sudden tingling sensation in his horns, he would have dropped off into a deep sleep again.

'But something is stirring,' he thought. 'Something that needs investigating.' Water dripped from his back, as he rose gracefully from the lake. "Bye ladies," he called to the Water-Lilly-spirits, "nature calls."

*

Brude nervously paced backward and forward outside his home. He had tried to stay seated on the boulder near the entrance, but he kept jumping up at every sound that came from within the dwelling. Finally, came the sound that he had so long waited to hear. From within the hollow of the tree a baby's first cry was heard. 'Taken breath has it?' beamed Brude, the Seeder of the child. His middle-aged face turned to panic though, when the birther ran out of the house.

'I'm sorry,' she thought, 'forgive me.'

Brude rushed inside to find the love of his life still kneeling on the birth stool, staring at the baby. Volas was trying to communicate with him using her mind, but her thoughts were in too much of a turmoil. He calmly picked up the Carnelian stone that she had dropped and put it in his pocket. "Use speech my love," he said, walking over to her side.

On looking at the baby boy's soft pale skin, something from within told him not to wrap it in the usual Pictish manner. He looked around for an alternative, and saw the cloth that Volas had received as a gift. The baby was a strange sight indeed. Its skin was like gossamer, and Brude could even see the blood flowing through its veins.

He gently covered the baby in the fabric that had come from a human village, and helped her to lay back on a bed of straw. It was then that he saw them; two cloven hooves at the end of a beam of light, followed by a goaty-bearded face; which had eyes like flames, and two small horns.

Pan popped his head around the entrance to the tree. This was one time when Brude welcomed one of Pan's intrusions, so he beckoned him to enter. Pan strolled in, his feet crunching on the graveled floor as he did so, and took the baby in his arms. He started to inspect the child, whilst Brude looked anxiously on. Both of them looked at each other when Pan discovered tiny bumps beneath the hairline, like little horn stumps. "Don't look at me," whispered Pan to Brude.

"Little Button-Nose," said Pan to Volas, "you have a very healthy and beautiful baby." She said nothing. He wanted to disperse the melancholy atmosphere as soon as possible. "Apart from its size and, oh, look at those ears, it looks more human than Pict." Pan's disarming smile and charm was able to make both Volas and Brude feel more calm. They had both seen this before with their friend. They also knew, but had never experienced it themselves, that he had a much darker side. Although seen as a male by many, Pan was in fact both male and female. Pan is nature, and nature must always keep its balance.

"He," whispered Volas, "it is a 'he', a poika, you old goat." Neither of them were quite sure who she had intended the comment for.

Pan suspected that a little magic had played a part in these proceedings. "Have you been carrying around the Carnelian stone that your visitor gave you?" asked Pan.

She nodded. "I needed help to conceive," she said, unapologetically.

Pan's expression was one of complete understanding. "And you rubbed on the tincture which he left for you as well?"

"Yes," she replied, knowing full well that she had both their support.

"You have done well Volas, for his magic is older than the world itself. He was here before even me. I also know that he visited the Finnic maidens, and a human he also helped. Rest now and do not worry. All will be well with the child," said Pan.

The silence was soon broken. "There is another one," they heard the birther scream.

Brude rushed outside. 'Silly creature,' he thought, as his normally rosy cheeks lost their colour. A female figure was seen rushing away from the birther. 'Poor thing,' thought Brude when he saw her running. Beneath the bushes another child had been born, and it was now screaming. Screaming in fear. He had to get to the baby; there was no time to stop the mother. Brude ran as fast as he could and cradled the baby in his arms. The boy's pulse was very weak. Its little fingers curled around Brude's finger and then held it in a vice-like grip. He saw the blood slowing in the veins and felt its warm beating heart flutter for just a moment, and then stop. The little hand gently released its grip. The baby sighed with its final breath.

Pan now stood behind Brude. "Let me see what I can do," said Pan.

*

Being used to mainly Moonlight for most of their lives, the Taezali couldn't cope with a sudden change to Sunlight. A lack of Moonlight led to a depression of the mind in some. As such, any child that showed signs of the sun-madness was kept in the Gap far longer than the other children. One of those children, Malceni, had been born only minutes after Lutrin. Brude had found him dead nearby. No Pict should be born in direct Sunlight. Luckily enough, help was at hand.

Pan had massaged the baby's undamaged heart and gave him the kiss of life. Neither the sun-madness nor the pain of abandonment could be healed quickly; although he did prescribe extract of yellow wort. Volas had to wet-nurse Malceni as well as her own son Lutrin.

***

Almost sixteen years after the birth of her son Lutrin, and adopted son Malceni, Volas was watching Lutrin playing. As many carers felt, she was both proud of his abilities and yet concerned for his future. That word "future" played havoc with her tura. The future had not been a great cause of concern for the Picts until recent times. However, as a wise-healer within the Taezali tribe it was one of the time-passages that she must consider.

Since she had given birth though, she began to wish that she led the simpler life of Senga, her womb-sharer, who would milk the cows and collect herbs for the wise-healers. Life had become "different" - an annoying word she thought, as was the word "annoying." A language, using spoken words instead of images with their turas, had drifted in with the ether from the world outside of Bryhery Gap.

Even Brude, the head carer and Seeder of her son, was now being called "King" Brude. Many of the tribes began to learn how to speak these words and a few had even started to "write" them down. This did not have the same "sound" or project the same picture onto a Pict's tura and, as such, some could not read or write these new symbols.

She hoped that a time would come when she could help those who could not cope with this difference, or inability to see languages that were not from the blood-line. Even she had problems. When her son was learning to write, he asked why was the letter 'g' written, but not pronounced, in many of the Babel tongue's words. Also why, if the letter 'i' was at the end of a word, was it pronounced "ee," unless after 'c.' "Such is the way of humans," was all she could offer.

Whilst Brude was away, visiting the Gridolers, Volas was sitting on a wooden stool outside the same tree which was always provided for them when they passed this way. An abundant supply of provisions had been left inside, and it had been cleaned and fresh straw laid out for their bedding. Today, Volas turned her attention to repairing the tribal tapestry. 'Lutrin. Come here, and tell me what is wrong with this,' she projected. The youngster didn't hear her; he was daydreaming. This was typical of many Picts who were not yet bonded to another, for although they grow older they would never lose their child-like imagination. "Lu," she called, "Lu, come here and tell me what you think is wrong with this."

On hearing his mother's call, he ran up the side of the embankment and knelt beside her as she stared at the fabric. Lutrin was very different from the other children.

He had very dark eyes, blonde hair and the chiseled features of a Finn. His skin was much lighter and softer than the usual dark grey and leathery texture of a Pict, and so Brude often called him 'Lutrin the Lucid'.

'Thank goodness he has at least stopped growing,' she thought.

Lutrin tried to ignore the remark. He had heard these kind of thoughts before from many other Taezali. Most Picts turas were not fully developed until they were as tall as the three foot Turoe stone of Ru. At forty-two inches Lutrin was the tallest Pict in Bryhery Gap. His tura was fully developed at an early age. The tribe had welcomed his differences and, at Brude's suggestion, they invited those less fortunate children from other tribes who were similar to Lutrin, to join them.

Although their skin was 'softer,' nevertheless they were still a hardy bunch. However, it did mean that their tunics had to be made from wool, lined with linen, rather than the bark extract that would have irritated their skin. Cow hides were overlaid on the wool. This had been the advice from Pan. He said that these children were delicate, like human children, and could catch illnesses very easily if they weren't covered up properly.

The main differences, between these children and the ordinary Picts, were that they had a full head of hair, had wide (not fat) hairy feet and possessed a different kind of "magic." Usually bald, Picts could, when required, assimilate various fungal growths over their outer skin. Indeed, most opted for a growth over the soles of their feet and the palms of their hands.

They could appear to be made of stone if they wished and nobody could tell the difference. By contrast, Lutrin and the other adopted children could mingle with any natural background, but could easily be discovered if you stood on them.

Unusually, Malceni had much darker skin than the others. With jet-black hair and the more 'rounded' features of a Gridoler, he looked more akin to the Picts recent ancestors, the Firbolgs.

Lutrin however, was also unique in that he had two very small deer-like velvet horns, and slightly pointed ears. Volas felt responsible for the way he looked. For a while, many maidens had problems conceiving children. A man came amongst them. At least, he looked human until you had a better chance to have a good look at him; for 'Tibias' kept changing his shape and appearance. He told many of them that they should carry a Carnelian stone in their tunics. In addition, he supplied a tincture and some incense made from: Mistletoe; white Oak bark; Thyme; Rue; Bay-leaves; Red Sandal Wood; Jasmine flowers; Cinnamon; Ginger and Lavender. A year later, it wasn't just Picts who saw the results of Tibias' magic, the Finns and a human had been touched too.

Lutrin continued to stare at the tapestry, which outlined the history of the Taezali. The tapestry would also 'change' of its own accord, revealing the current nature and feelings of the community. 'There are gaps between the threads,' he observed.

'But why are there gaps?'

'Because the' "friends" 'have separated.'

At the word "friend" she flinched. Lutrin had spoken it out loud rather than thinking it and projecting it onto her tura. He had developed a habit of mixing the two. She was worried that he was becoming too comfortable with the spoken word. It was after all the language of loneliness, whereas the Pict tura was total sharing. Reverting to speech, she said, "Why are the friends parting?"

"I don't know," he replied with a hurt expression on his face, as if he should have known the answer.

"It is because there is a beast arising from the outside. It is all devouring, and will one day affect us deeply. I am telling you this now because I envisage a hitherto unforeseen future bound up with a new age of events."

The idea of a quest to find the beast excited him a little. "And what is the name of this beast?"

"Alas, I can not see it for it has many heads with different names."

"If it bothers our tribe so much then I promise you that one day I shall find the name of this beast for you." He paused and looked down at his feet. "I see more with my tura than I like to see. This is why I often talk too much." He was clearly very distressed and began to visibly shake.

Volas hoped that Lutrin wasn't going to have one of his 'episodes'. She knew how to handle them because it was only an illusion that he projected, but to some nearby it could be quite frightening. In his early years, Lutrin's tura was so well developed that any nightmares which he experienced, were projected to all those around him. It was the centaur, Panara, who had taught Lutrin to use his lips, and she helped to sooth his fears.

"Then speak to me in anyway that enables you to communicate freely with me. For I would rather have a talking son than a turaless Pict."

"The outside world is aware of our existence. They will come one day and I fear for you my mother. I saw into the mind of the Orci in Orcades. They say a healer is a witch."

Using his tura, he began to show her the image of the Orci. The terrain was a fairly flat area shaped like a star, and at its centre was a dark lake. Within this, men and women were throwing rocks at a poor old woman and, when she looked close to death, they tied a large stone to her and dropped her into the lake.

When Lutrin spoke and projected at the same time, it was almost like being physically present. In many ways it was more real because he also magnified the emotions of those he saw.

"Kill the witch," they shouted and, with every rock they threw, "die, die, die."

Lutrin then whispered, "and from now on it will always be so." Volas' face turned a deathly pale colour. Her stomach churned as she felt both the terrifying fear of the old woman's last moments and the pleasure the people were having. How could he see so far from the Gap?

"That is not all. Far to the rising of the Moon I saw a great cliff between the land and a narrow gap of water. Humans were nearby. Probing. Always probing for a way in. And then a mighty catastrophe. All change." At this point he broke down and refused to communicate normally. He was even able to close off his tura.

Volas didn't know it, but Lutrin did this so as to shield her from the picture he had of the terrifying 'Blood Eagle' ritual, performed by the Orci on the leaders of the people they conquered.

The following week he used only "telepathy" when he wanted to speak. This was a type of speech that was considered to be crude, because it projected only the words of speech into someone else's mind – and not onto their tura. The other children copied him, thinking it was fun at first, and then adopted its use long after.

*

The King of the Picts was on his way to visit the Gridolers. He liked these moments to himself. In the Bryhery Gap, everyone knew exactly what everyone else was thinking. As he journeyed on, the Tajem forest got ever closer to the shoreline as he neared the Eyribol Ridge. Along the coast at Eyribol however, no trees whatsoever grew and few Picts resided there. Brude briefly stepped onto the Eyribol Ridge before heading in a sharp south-easterly direction into Gridoler territory.

On his journey through the mountains, Brude was accompanied by Panara; a white centaur with dark-brown eyes and a small horn on her head. When no other centaurs from Panara's race where present, she permitted Brude to ride on her back. This was something centaurs usually only allowed young Picts to do. Panara bore him over each little river, through bracken, briar and heather, and up to the mouth of a cave on the peak of the biggest mountain. He dismounted and entered the cave, which was hidden behind a curtain of water.

A young Gridoler whom Brude recognised, had been sent to wait for him. Raven led him through a series of tunnels that wound their way down into the mountain-side. As he passed through these tunnels, with much concern he noted that a number of mine shafts had filled up with salt water.

Eventually, he entered the comfortable chambers of Chief Deedle Wilde. "May your beard grow ever longer and your gold ever brighter," said the King, employing a traditional Gridolic greeting which he had used many times before.

Deedle, revealing his own word-hoard, politely replied, "And may your tree ever face the Moon." He paused, and then continued to say, "Brude, Raven tells me there is a good mist over the mountain."

He nodded. In spite of the long journey, he preferred to get his business over with before engaging in social chat. "Something is wrong here Deedle," said Brude, "I saw the water in the tunnels; it is not natural." He slowly eased himself down onto a chair carved into the side of the chamber. The hollow looked quite ancient but everything was in fact relatively new.

Deedle was a pleasant enough chap. Dressed in bright green trousers with a light brown coat, he looked more of a king than Brude, who always wore a grey knee length tunic woven from plants and the inner bark of a tree. Brude's attire was really quite typical of many Picts. "We found some beautiful caves and wanted to enlarge the caverns," began Deedle enthusiastically, "but perhaps we dug too deep."

"But sea water Deedle, sea water. If salt comes onto the land we could all be in trouble; for a start, it would rot the Tajem root. Your love of Blue-John will ruin us all."

Raven entered the chamber and placed slices of pig and cow on the table in front of Brude.

"No. No. Bring the special grits prepared by Pliny," hissed an embarrassed Deedle. Brude showed no sign of offence, so Raven left quickly.

"As for the Blue-John," said Deedle, "you tax enough of it yourself from us. Besides, it may not have been our fault; for some time now, we have felt the earth shaking from within".

It was Pliny herself who returned with some fish, fruit, a tiny bowl of powdered granite and two mugs of ale. Brude indicated his thanks and proceeded to sprinkle some of the powder on the fish. Deedle was always fascinated with this part of the Picts' diet. Having initially questioned the reason for this, it had been explained that the powdered granite was sprinkled on the Pict's food in order to ensure that they didn't lose their ability to 'become as stone'.

(Pliny was Deedle's snuggler. She had long, flowing, curly golden hair down to her ankles, as did all Gridolets. Although Gridolers had no hair, except for their beards, the Gridolets were very proud of their long hair and hairy legs, which they combed regularly.)

"Don't worry," continued Deedle, "we have measured the depth of the chamber and have set that as our mining limit." "We have known each other a long time Deedle. I accept your word. Now, where is my Blue-John; my food can wait till later."

(It is hard to stay angry for long with a Gridoler, because of a little natural magic that they innocently and unconsciously use. When a person sees something unpleasant in someone, it can often be a reflection of their own faults that they see. When looking at a Gridoler however, the opposite is true. The result is, not only do you know that it was your own failing which you saw, but you also think the Gridoler is quite the opposite.)

As Deedle led Brude to an adjacent chamber he paused. "Brude. I truly do not intend to be rude, but what need does your race have for this precious stone?"

"I am sure it does seem strange, but 'change' is coming, and I fear that my people could suffer from it. If I have something that the outside world wants then we will be stronger for it; I am not aware of any other place, anywhere in the world that has this stone."

"Not wishing to devalue it my Lord Brude, but I should say that it is rumored that our mine is but a small shadow of the undiscovered true source of the Blue-John. There is a story that says my people came from a hole in the ground next to 'Mam Tor'."

"The Shivering Mountain?" Asked Brude.

Deedle nodded. "On seeing daylight for the first time my ancestors sought refuge in the nearest cave possible. On entering it they discovered a wonderful seam of blue and yellow stone with flashes of white. Much of that can not be taken literally of course. But what happened next is fact.

The Finns, having never seen our race before, thought that we were some terrible creatures from the underworld. They chased us out of Belevedon, all the way from the mountain, which is east of the Eyribol Ridge, until we went underground where you now find us. As the stone is so scarce, we think that this mine is just the end of a seam emanating from that much larger source."

"I have a feeling," said Brude, "the Finns knew precisely what they were doing. Did they slay any of your kin"?

"Why, no. We were too quick for them."

"Deedle, rest assured that they must have wanted it so; for none of us are too quick for the Finnic."

"Ah, here we are."

Surveying the storage units, Brude continued, "Looking at this beautiful sight almost makes me regret my harsh words; I say 'almost' mind. Keep this with all of the prior shipments and I will collect it on my way to the next Athelney meeting. Until then, add all future shipments to it as well. I will not make further inspections until that time."

"Within a few years, that hoard would be enough to buy a new land. Why take it to Athelney?"

Brude laughed a little, "A King must be allowed to have some secrets. Tell only those that need to make the preparations. At that time, I would like to hire some of your people as hoard-watchers. I want it all placed in a cavern near Athelney. They may remain there for a couple of years, but I will reward them handsomely."

"I will make it so, but only if you also inform the Finns of your plan."

"They already know."

Shortly after Brude had left, a young Gridoler entered Deedle's chamber. Tilli was the only Gridoler who chose to have a short goaty-beard, similar to Pan. He was also slimmer than most of his kind and had control over his eyelid contractions.

"Hello young Tilli. What news brings you so far West?"

Tilli entered the room and removed his cap. "Our latest estimates show that the great tunnel is now but a few years from completion."

"Excellent," said Deedle pouring him a cup of water, "and the western route?"

"It should be ready within the year," said a rather pleased looking Tilli. Despite his desire to gulp the water down in one go, Tilli sipped it politely.

"A year," Deedle replied, almost as if he was disappointed, "well done, in that case shift all but the most essential maintenance staff onto the great tunnel instead."

"Consider it so."

"Please be seated," said Deedle. Tilli sat in the chair previously occupied by Brude, and Deedle sat back in his chair, smiling to himself. "Things are going better than I thought. Soon we may get back what is rightfully ours."

"That will be a glorious day my Chief. One worthy of a song."

"Yes, a song that will echo through the ages." He liked Tilli very much. 'You shall take my place one day,' he thought. "Tilli, do you have a snuggler yet?"

"No. I have been too busy with my work."

"A pity. After you have relayed my orders I want you to take time to choose one. Go and play the joy-game of marriage. And while you are at it, cultivate other interests. You are far too clever to just be my messenger."

"That would be marvelous," he replied, standing up to leave.

"No, sit. I would like you to stay for supper. We have much to discuss, and Pliny would welcome one of your stories."

Tilli could see it was going to be a long night.

Chapter 2: **EYRIBOL**

The nomadic Taezali tribe were blessed with long life because they lived in what was known as the Bryhery Gap. The Gap moved with them or rather they moved with the Gap. During the daytime the Moon was always full and, throughout the month, it was the Sun which waxed and waned. This phenomena was a reflection of the world from which their spirits had once come from; the world on the other side of the Bryhery Gap. To keep in step with the turning of the Great Wheel, they would walk about nineteen miles once every Full Sun and stay there for roughly twenty-nine days. The Gap's own sphere of influence had a diameter of nineteen miles. The hub of the Zali's wheel was located on the isle of Manni, Lord of the Moon, in the centre of the Island in the centre of a great lake. No Pict had travelled the swan-road there in Pictish memory. However, Brude knew that the Finns visited it. The reason why, was one question that he intended to one day find the answer to.

'This will be a hot summer,' thought Brude, as he rode Panara back from the mountains and closer to home.

"Lu knows nothing of his future life yet then?"

Panara hadn't spoken for some time and the spoken word surprised him, bringing him quickly out of his daydream.

"Of course not," said Brude, "he is far too young to know."

"I can not go with him," she said sadly.

They could faintly hear the sound of children's laughter in the distance.

"I know, and I know it will break his heart. You are his best friend Panara. Without you he may never have spoken as a child. As it turned out we both know how important that was."

"It will also break my heart. At times like this I almost wish I was not a mythical creature."

Brude dismounted. "Alas, poor Panara, but that is what you are." Her image began to dissolve.

"See you later," she whispered, and then was gone.

At the bottom of the hill, the Taezali were gathering at the start of the Eyribol Ridge. In years past they would carry all of their belongings on their backs. Nowadays though, everything was put in carts and the cows would pull them. Their monthly encampments were also different. Except for when they were on the Ridge, there was no more camping out or living in relatives tree houses for the month. Today, the Taezali rested in trees that had been made temporarily vacant. When Brude became carer of the Picts, he told all the stationary Picts that it was only right that they provide homes for the passing Taezali.

Many of the older Picts did not relish the next two months in this area. They always arrived in Summer of course, but there was still very little for the young ones to do, so they would go on ahead to Ru. This meant eight weeks outside of the Gap for the children; they would also age a little on the outside. Some, like Malceni, were not permitted to leave the Gap at all, because they were prone to the sun-madness. Lutrin was permitted to go, but felt sorry for Malceni. As such, Lutrin with the help of Panara was the only child who went in and out of the Gap all summer long.

Still at the top of the hill, Brude looked to his left. In the near distance he could see the sea, and to his right was the great lake. The rolling sea waves looked wild and threatening, whereas the Lake was peaceful and welcoming. Only Eyribol stood between the two. How long would this last he thought. Surely much longer than the northern ice-cap. But so what. When one of them gave-way, much of Sunna would be lost beneath the water. What was left would be split in two, and the Island would also be split. 'Well, not this day,' he thought, 'not this day,' and made his way down to wish the children farewell.

The air was full of excitement as the children packed last minute bits and pieces. They looked forward to arriving in Ru for what they always saw as a holiday. Lutrin, who had recently celebrated his sixteenth birthday, was the first to greet Brude. "Seeder," he shouted.

This did not surprise him, for Lutrin was a loving child.

'And to think,' thought Brude, before Lutrin was in hearing range, 'that some folk thought he was a freak when he was born. Thank goodness Malceni arrived soon after to show it was otherwise.'

'Are you all set to go?' thought Brude to Lutrin.

"Yes," replied Lutrin, looking straight into his father's eyes.

'Use your tura,' rebuked Brude.

'Sorry Seeder,' thought Lutrin, 'I am ready.'

'Good.' Brude closed his eyes and concentrated on Lutrin's mind, 'Here is Panara.'

Lutrin turned to see Panara standing behind him. "Ready for some summer fun little Lu?" she asked.

Brude frowned at her excessive use of human speech, but said no more. It had been vital for Lutrin as an infant, but he had hoped that his son wouldn't become so reliant on it.

"Yes," said Lutrin, "but I am not so little anymore. Perhaps I am too grown up to continue riding you?"

"Perhaps you are. I will be going then," she teased.

Lutrin rushed forward and held on to her long black hair. "Just for a while then," she said laughing.

He leapt onto her back and, without any further goodbyes, they galloped away onto the Eyribol Ridge.

'I shouldn't be so hard on him,' pondered Brude, 'because of his size, I forget he is still young. But I must speak to Volas about this speech he is so fond of.'

Panara slowed to a trot because she had built up quite a steam, and eventually came to a stop. She loved being in this dimension. For good reasons, Panara had exceptionally long silky-black hair, and had become accustomed to pulling it over the front of her shoulders and then combing it regularly.

Lutrin startled her from her thoughts. "Please take me to the sea Panara."

Together, they passed through the vale of the Gap and entered a world of hot sunshine, scented flowers and gentle salt sea breezes. The Sun changed places with the Moon. Lutrin had to cover his eyes at first. It was such a hot day that Lutrin rolled the top of his tunic down around his waist.

As they trotted on past a group of Picts who had departed from the main group earlier, they exchanged greetings.

A few minutes later as they approached the only accessible pathway to the beach, they heard a great deal of shouting. Lutrin dismounted, knocking a large stone over the cliff with his foot as he did so, and peered over the edge of the cliff.

On the beach, an old man lay unconscious on the sand. In front of him stood a few tall shining people. "Panara, look. See the Urs waiting for the old man's last breath?"

"No," she said, "they are the Finns. See their sharp swords. Hear their arrows sing." The arrows were aimed at four long-boats containing many fearsome looking men.

"We must help them Lutrin."

"Help who, the Ur..Finns or the men in boats?"

"You decide," she said, testing his powers of discernment.

"The Finns?"

"Good lad. Now go on."

Lutrin didn't move. "Oh. Yes, but ... I sense danger, for you."

"I am not really here. I can not die."

"I know you say so ... but ... I am afraid for you. My horns are tingling."

She stroked his horns gently; reminding herself of how she used to help him get to sleep during the night of a Full Sun.

"Mine is too Lu," she said, "but we must try. Come. Now."

It was an old crumbling track that led them down to the beach. Lutrin tripped over twice in haste. On reaching the beach, they saw the old man open his deep blue eyes. Eyes that matched the colour of his cloak. Lutrin noticed a distant starry look in them, but couldn't quite recall what it was that he saw.

"Begone poika quickly, get the centaur away from here. A Pict should know better than to meddle in the affairs of a wizard."

"But meddle I will," he said, helping the man to his feet and retrieving his staff, "what is your name?"

"My name is Amergin." He staggered a little, and sat down on a boulder to wipe the sand from his face and the dust off his cloak. "Oh, I am too weak for battle. Tell the Finns to retreat."

Lutrin said nothing. Impatiently, the wizard muttered a few words and the Finns began to back up.

"You can not stop now," Lutrin said, "there are children up there".

The Finns began firing more arrows down onto the boats; in most cases hitting only the men's shields. Then came a body blow to Lutrin, or rather Panara. An enormous spear hit her so hard that it almost went right through her. Her front legs gave way beneath her and she fell to the ground. She tried to stand up again, but her head rolled sickly to one side. The colour of the golden sand was now red.

"No," screamed Lutrin.

"Goodbye Lu," she said.

As he looked one last time into her eyes, he saw all that was beautiful and good in the world encompassed in her gaze. Then, her eyes glazed over and she was gone. Panara's body faded from sight, and Lutrin held his head in his hands.

'They still have the smell of her hair on them,' he thought, 'it's funny what you think of when you lose someone.'

"Get a move on poika. You can't bring her back." The wizard's attitude left much to be desired.

"But she is not dead. She has only returned to her own dimension."

"That is true poika, but once killed in this reality she can't visit it anymore. You knew that when you brought her down her. It is ... is, against the rules for her to come back."

A grief-racked Lutrin turned to face the invaders. His eyes tore into them, and both they and the Finns stopped dead in their tracks as he did so. He held up his hands. Those present were about to witness a demonstration of a Pict's' 'tura'. A 'tura', normally used to mentally communicate pictures and feelings to other Picts, could also be used to project those images onto the minds of any person nearby.

"You will fear me," Lutrin shouted angrily.

The water around the ships began to boil, sending up a mist which surrounded his enemy. The mist became black and the boats could no longer be seen. Deep from within the mist came many terrifying screams.

A light breeze blew across the sand and dispersed the mist; revealing an unconscious mass of men. Their hair had gone grey and their facial expressions were contorted with fear.

"They will leave here, for the time being," said Lutrin calmly, "but go and rescue the captive."

During Lutrin's outburst, he noticed that there was someone in the boat who was obviously not a warrior, and so he made sure that the illusion had no effect on him.

"He is right. Look," said said one of the Finns, "on the boat." He ran forward and found a young man, who was a little older than Lutrin, tied up.

'Bound for slavery?' thought Lutrin.

'Yes. Help me please,' he replied.

'A telepathic human,' thought Lutrin, as the teenager was lifted gently from the boat. He had blistered bare feet, which explained why he winced when he was set down upon the hot sand.

"Take him back to his own people," said Amergin, "I must go home and rest."

As the human walked past Lutrin he stopped. Lutrin felt his fear. "Thank you. I hope someday to help you in return," he said.

Lutrin noticed that he had long hair with a ribbon tied to it. However, just as he was about to utter his name, Amergin interjected, "No. You have seen too much of each other already. The time-line must not be affected. Go."

As the Finns left with the human, known as Taesus, the wizard turned to Lutrin, "I came to rescue the poika. You were not meant to be here ... I think. As I reached the beach a huge rock fell on my head; that was your work I presume. This is most odd; all of us here today were meant to meet at some point in the future, but not today."

A downbeat Lutrin started to walk away. "I have no time for your rantings. I must tell my Seeder what has happened."

The wizard had to block off his mind from the Pict. 'He's giving up a little too soon,' he thought. "The Finns will tell him sooner than you can. Go back up and enjoy yourself," he said.

Lutrin stopped. He was disorientated and lost. More tears came to his eyes. "But how can I ... with ... without my Panara?"

'That's better,' thought Amergin. "There is a way. It is cheating a little," he said. The wizard dropped his mental block and pictured Panara when she was younger. Then the block came back up.

"I can imagine her ... yes ... imagine her 'before' she first met me". Within moments a younger Panara appeared next to Lutrin. "Panara," he cried, overjoyed.

"You know me?" a somewhat bewildered Panara enquired, her eyes soft as ever, but lacking any recognition of the delighted Lutrin.

"Yes. No. Oh, just come on. I will tell you all about it later ... oh, er ... some other day," Lutrin replied, accepting with gratitude the loss experienced as infinitely preferable to its alternative.

Lutrin and Panara reached the Ridge just as the Picts they had passed earlier caught up with them.

The wizard was, for the time being, quite perplexed. It was a condition which he was unused to. He felt the knife in his pocket, and remembered the other reason why he went to the beach that day. He ran after the Finns to complete his mission.

Chapter 3: **BRYHERY GAP**

On the opposite side of the ridge, about nine weeks later, Lutrin went to peer through a hedge and spy on the faeries. Panara appeared behind him. "Would you like to meet Pan?" she said.

"What world does he live in?" asked Lutrin, thinking it was time for another story. She always did this when he was 'being serious' as she called it. But then he remembered that this younger Panara had not told him any stories yet.

"Why this one of course. Pan never left. Pan could not leave. Pan is nature. He was here two Moons ago, just before we met, but you were too preoccupied to notice him. Pictish children usually see him as soon as they open their eyes."

His initial reaction was to say, 'But I am not a proper Pict am I?' But he was getting too old for that now, besides, what she had said intrigued him. "Who is Pan?"

"He is a spirit," continued Panara, "who combines the male-tree and the female-fauna energies within the animal. He can be seen in the earth, heard on the wind and felt in the water." When she said things like that, there was usually a moral or a lesson to learn.

"And what about fire?" asked Lutrin, showing his enthusiasm for anything that Panara said.

"Ask me that yourself and the answers will come much faster." Lutrin heard the crunch of hooves on stone, and turned to see a two-legged man-shaped creature with pointed ears. He had the lower legs of a horse with the upper legs and stomach of a deer. His chest and arms were human but upon his head were two velvet-covered horns. The horns were considered small, but were obviously much larger than Lutrin's. It was Pan. "This is quite a combination you chose for my appearance," he said, patting his hands on his legs.

Lutrin thought this was an unusual looking creature, certainly nothing he would have dreamt up. "What do you mean?"

"In a fully animal shaped form it is the viewer who creates the myth. Some people give me goats legs. I presume that you picked a horse because you know that Panara is my daughter."

"What?" howled Lutrin rudely, laughing.

"He did not know father. We have only just met."

He stared down into Lutrin's eyes. 'Was that a flame in his eyes,' thought Lutrin, 'and did he say, "what a tangled web we weave when first we practice to deceive".' He felt as if Pan was examining his very soul.

"Let us get back to fire. Animals do not use fire; I did not know fire until I had union with people. Peoples consciousness leapt when they discovered fire," said Pan. "People do not know this, but you see, together, people and I can change reality. The inner sacred-fire that you bring to my elements will act like a conduit; it can send a signal outside the fields of potentiality that created this world to change the original thought pattern of this universe. But enough of this. Would you like to meet Panara's mother?"

"Why yes. But how. I thought that they had removed themselves far from our world."

"'This' world," corrected Pan, "not 'our' world. The Unicorns' dimension is indeed far away. But any existence, any place, is never too far from Bryhery Gap. Come, let me show you a secret of the Gap. A secret that most of the Taezali do not even know they protect."

Pan led Lutrin to the edge of the Bryhery vale and down to the lake shoreline. "Now Lutrin, look at the water and tell me what you see." Lutrin stared long and hard, but all he could see was the light shimmering on the surface of the water. "You can't see the wood for the trees can you?" laughed Pan. "In the light there are many colours. Stop looking at the spectrum as one; look instead at the individual parts."

As Lutrin looked once more, he began to see individual beams of light. "It is beautiful," he said.

"Yes," confirmed Pan, "but there is more here than just a pretty sight. Look at one colour only."

Lutrin looked deep into the colour yellow. From there he saw more shades of yellow, and within those shades even more strands of colour. "Good," said Pan, "now touch a single thread. Just one."

As Lutrin touched it, there was a flash. The single colour just exploded in size to reveal a bridge. A bridge of light. "Well done. Well done Lutrin." His heart was pounding fast. He had never seen anything like this before. Without any hesitation Lutrin stepped forward. "Stop," said Pan. Lutrin froze in fear. "Relax Lu, I'm not going to eat you. I'm here to help you. Now, where does the bridge lead to?"

Lutrin looked down at his feet. He was about to tell Pan about the boulders on the other side, but instead he said, "I thought we would explore, that is all."

Pan continued, "Chin up. That bridge could lead anywhere. Anywhere in time and space. You must project your tura over the bridge first. What you should do is practice, as often as you can, and learn about the light. Then you will be as free as Panara and I." He waved his hand and the bridge was gone. "Okay," he said, creating another bridge, "let us go and see the Unicorns."

They both stepped onto the bridge and crossed over it, into a world of thick colours. What surprised Lutrin was that the trees and plants looked ancient. "Remember," said Pan, "when they left your reality they chose a dimension more fitting for themselves. Now, keep very quiet and I will call them." Pan took up the pipes which he had tied around his waist and began to play.

Lutrin could almost see the notes and the melody drift in the air. Closing his eyes, he felt relaxed, peaceful and happy. So happy that he didn't hear the Unicorns arrive.

"Here she is, and with her mate too," said Pan.

"But I thought ..."

"Nay, nay, nay," replied Pan, expressing the sound in a very horse-like manner. "You do need some education. Centaurs are only given life by those who love them. Panara is the union of spirit." He grinned and pointed at himself. "That's me," he said. "And the physical." He pointed at the Unicorns. "That's them."

Lutrin looked very puzzled, so Pan continued, "You need to learn more about magical creatures Lutrin. Centaurs are mythical, whereas Unicorns really do physically exist. However, to be fair, Panara is different because she does physically exist when she is here, with them." Lutrin went to stroke one of them. "No," interjected Pan, "do not corrupt them."

Lutrin nodded. "Thank you for showing me how to use the Gap." Walking back to the bridge he stopped and turned to Pan. "Are you not coming?"

Pan laughed. "The bridge is for you Lu. I am already there remember. I am everywhere, at all times and in all places."

*

Back in their own reality, Brude was waiting for Lutrin. "Lutrin," he said, "I know that Pan has been teaching you about Bryhery Gap. However, before he gets in with further pearls of knowledge, let me point out a few things for you. What you do not know about the light bridges that you can cross is that they have little to do with the Gap. You either have the ability to do that anywhere or you do not. As for the real purpose of the Gap, let me show you something."

They walked across the bog and into a secluded area surrounded by bushes. A large beech tree stood at the centre of the clearing.

"Now, look at those faeries over there," said Brude. "Tell me, have you ever bothered to talk to them? Talk to them properly I mean?" Lutrin shook his head. "I did not think so. Because you see them as everyday things, like the birds, mice and flowers. I tell you this, they are not.

They are mostly transient individuals between two worlds. You, we, were like them before we became Picts. Some will become Gridolers, some will become men and a few will remain as faeries."

Lutrin looked at the nearest group of faeries buzzing around the tree. They were so lovely that he found it difficult to imagine that some of them would actually choose to be Orci. They had a very simple intellect, with no knowledge of the outside world. They were the colour of mercury, had no bodily hair, or clothing, and had no outward appearance of gender. However, for some unknown reason, they did have faerie children. Faeries prefer to communicate with images, rather than words. They were also known to induce visions. They could visit the outside world, but their physicality was as a result of people. The greater the physical form attributed to them by humans, the easier the faeries could operate or change the form of their surroundings. Unconsciously, people knew this and, as such, preferred not to give them too much form because faery power could also transform that person's form as well.

"What happens to those who remain faeries?" asked Lutrin.

"As you know, the Gap lies between two worlds, the one we came from and the one we are going to. It is we that choose when and where we want to go. The Gap is a place to rest. Many faeries who stay like that do so because they are either afraid of being born again or did not survive their new birth. So, they prefer to stay a little longer before choosing their next life. But remember, we can also, if we wish, go home again. Back to where we first came from."

Chapter 4: **MANNI**

It was Lutrin and Malceni's eighteenth birthday. It was also a glorious mid-summer day, and three Finns had just arrived at the centre of the Eyribol Ridge. With every move they made, the sunlight was magnified as it reflected off their skin. The leader of the Finns wore a tunic, but the others wore trousers and a half-tunic. Both types of clothing were made from a mixture of cloth, like humans use, and plant materials. They were so exquisitely sown together that it was not possible to see where the leaves and bark were joined to the cloth.

One of the Finns noticed how Lutrin admired his half-tunic. "It is just as well little Master, that you like our attire. For Brude has exchanged cows for many of them; so that you and your kind may have clothes more suitable for your outlook," said Tarquin.

Aniel, the leader of the Finns, and Uriel, walked towards Brude. "Greetings Aniel. It is always a great pleasure when you visit my country, on your way to Manni," he said, raising a hairless eyebrow questioningly.

Aniel smiled, and his long bushy eyebrows fluttered in the wind, "The pleasure is ours also."

"May I ask, why do you visit Manni?"

"Amergin, a lord of time, lives on Manni. We often seek his counsel."

"I met him down on the beach a few years ago," said Lutrin enthusiastically.

"That is not possible," said Aniel, peering down his long nose at Lutrin, "Amergin does not leave Manni anymore. That explains why you once told me that Amergin handed you over to Norbold the Orci corpse-maker. You must have been mistaken, perhaps ... ."

"I am sorry sir," interrupted Lutrin, "but I have never met you before this day. I assure you that I know nothing of what you speak."

"There is truth in your eyes poika," said a puzzled Aniel.

"And also in yours Aniel," said Brude, "so, something very wrong is going on."

"We should ask Amergin," said Aniel, "and Lutrin should come with us."

"Do you think that it is wise?" They all turned to see Lutrin's friend, Malceni, approaching.

"Your opinion was not looked for little Pict," said Aniel, grinning at the boldness of the youth.

"If I go, Malceni is coming too," said Lutrin.

"I agree with Lutrin," said Brude, "but 'Play it by ear,' as the Gridolers would say." It was then that Lutrin noticed that Aniel had very long ears; twice the length of Tarquin's.

*

Unlike the steep cliffs on the seaside of the Ridge, the shoreline of the lake rose steadily to meet them. They boarded the Finns' boat and made headway towards Manni. Neither Lutrin nor Malceni had ever travelled so far into the great lake. Although it was summer, there was a cold wind blowing over the lake, and the Picts began to shiver.

"It will take us many hours to get there young Picts. Perhaps you should cover yourselves up?" said Tarquin.

"I could get us there much quicker by bridge." Lutrin had, in fact, had his eye on Manni for a while. He had practiced making bridges there, but had not actually gone yet.

The Finns smiled at one another, for the Picts were as children to their eyes. "And where might this bridge be," continued Tarquin.

"Why here of course," said Lutrin, pointing at the water.

In front of the boat, a bridge of light appeared. The bridge looked to both start and finish in the water.

"An impressive trick Lutrin," said Aniel, "but it will not get us very far."

"You do not understand. Watch. Come on Mal." Lutrin and Malceni jumped from the boat and onto the bridge. The Finns were taken aback. "Are you coming then?"

"Where?" Chorused the Finns.

"To Manni of course. It is just over here. Oh, forget it, we will see you later." Malceni and Lutrin walked over the bridge and onto Manni. Meanwhile, Tarquin and Uriel were in a panic. All they saw was that two Picts had walked across the water and then gone underneath it.

"Relax," said Aniel, "they clearly knew exactly what they were doing."

*

Now that Lutrin and Malceni were on Manni, they realised that they didn't actually know where on Manni they were supposed to go. They climbed up the nearest hill to get their bearings. As they did so they noticed an unpleasant smell of rotting flesh.

"Oh dear," said Lutrin mischievously, "look at those piles of dung next to the rotting meat. I know where we are!"

"What? What is it?" said Malceni nervously.

"Some say that a hideous creature, known as giant wood louse comes in the dead of night."

"Stop," said Malceni, "he is good person."

"Who? Who is a good person?" Asked Lutrin, screwing up his nose.

"The Woodwose of the Tajem forest. Not the wood louse. He is the oldest faery known to Brude."

"Okay then," he continued unabated, "but it is also said that Brude has an 'understanding,' with another, even bigger creature. Brude sets aside some meat for it, on the condition that it will help defend Sunna if we are ever attacked."

"Oh oh," said Malceni with fear in his eyes, "that is actually a true story."

"It is?" he replied worryingly.

"Yes. Brude feeds the last of the Roc's."

"I have a bad feeling about this."

As Lutrin finished speaking a shadow came over them. Their hearts were pounding fast as they heard a deep coughing sound. The eye of the giant Roc bird was on them, and its owner was about to pounce.

Malceni stood up, bowed to the Roc and started to speak. Lutrin had no idea what they were saying, but it was obviously going well. "Come on," said Malceni, "he is going to take us to Amergin."

"I do not believe it," said Lutrin.

"Well, they had to teach me something all that time the rest of you were out of the Gap. Your aunt Senga taught me to speak Roc. That is why we are able to fly to Amergin's instead of being eaten!"

The Roc headed for the peak of Snaefel mountain, and dropped them off outside the front door of an enormous castle. Before they could pull the bell, the door opened. Malceni thanked the Roc before they entered.

On stepping into the hallway, they heard a voice in the distance, "Aniel, welcome to Castle Sardit, come on in. You are early. Supper is far from ready."

They opened a door on their right and noticed that a window facing east was open, but nobody was there. So they checked out the door to their left and saw that a window facing west was also open. A man, who looked a little like Aniel with a closely-cropped beard, was looking out of the window. He turned on his heels. "Welcome I, .. oh, its you two. About ten years too soon!"

Lutrin looked in every direction. "Something is not right here," he said, "the castle is smaller on the inside than it is on the outside," said Lutrin.

"And why do think that is?" asked Amergin.

"I can not be certain," interjected Malceni, "but if the time-passage of this structure could be constricted, squashed if you like, into a tiny space, then the internal life-span curve would be exponentially extended." Lutrin and Amergin looked at him. "I told you I have been studying, things and stuff."

The wizard abruptly changed the subject. "Well, there it is," said Amergin, "on the lectern. It is your mirror. Just for you Lutrin. You will feel a bit odd as you mount the step but it is okay really." He turned and looked out of the window again.

"Are you always this rude?" said Malceni. Neither he nor Lutrin had any idea of the significance of the mirror.

"Only when I'm busy concentrating."

"You do not seem busy now." It was obvious that Malceni had not taken a shine to the wizard.

"You have no idea what I am doing," said Amergin as he glared at Malceni with his cold grey eyes.

"I have a tale to tell you," said Lutrin.

"Just the one? Go on then."

Lutrin told Amergin everything; about meeting him on the beach, and what Aniel had said about having seen Lutrin years earlier.

Aniel walked in just before he finished speaking.

"Lutrin, what have you done?" said a rather annoyed Aniel.

"Oh don't chastise the poika Aniel. You would have told me it all yourself over supper. It is this castle you see. I never meant to make it get the truth from people, but it's probably an after-affect of the time-differential."

"You know, the truth outs in the end and all that," quipped Malceni.

"Now, Amergin, what of our story?" asked Aniel.

"Firstly, I would like Lutrin to take his mirror from the lectern. Go on, it is quite safe."

Lutrin stepped up to the lectern and saw writing in the mirror, "The Tale of a Bryhery Pict, from 'Lucid'." He began to read out loud.

"In a tree, in a wood by a lake, lived a Pict. This was not just any old tree full of insects and rotting wood. For long, long ago – long before men had cut all the big trees down; the trees were so large and wide that a Pict could live in one very comfortably thank you. This particular tree house belonged to a famous 'evolved'-Pict. Famous for his adventures at the end of the alpha time-passage when evolved-Pict first met human and had dealings with the Finns; in particular the branch of Finns known as 'primordial-dwarf El-finns.' The new Pict and small Elfin races would only exist for one generation, but when fate brought them together their mixed-race off-spring created a new race. This is the true story of a Bryhery Pict, son of a white-witch. The name of Lutrin Zali's first child was ......"

"What does it say about me?" interrupted Malceni.

"Come away now Lutrin," said Amergin, "you have seen more than enough. You too Malceni."

"But what about me?" pleaded Malceni.

"That is enough."

"What was I looking at Amergin?," asked Lutrin.

"It is a time-line."

"You mean the future?"

"No, but it could be if you continue along a particular path."

"Why have you shown me this?"

"Because it is your mirror, or rather it is the missing mirror of the Picts. It was lent to me a long time ago and I, well ... let us say I forgot to give it back."

'Crafty,' thought Malceni.

"Crafty perhaps young Pict and best remembered by you." They had clearly got off to a bad start.

"How should I use it?", asked Lutrin.

"Very little for now. It is a precious artifact brought by Mithras to earth from before the heavens existed – he who thought your race into being. It was made by Mithras' evil brother Thoth. Three other brothers there were. All four oppose Thoth, but only Mithras is strong enough to kill him, and that is something he will not do. The youngest brother is more 'earthy' shall we say and is permitted to even try to destroy Thoth." A tear formed in Amergin's eye, so he paused and composed himself.

Meanwhile, Malceni slowly inched his way towards the lectern.

"Master Amergin, there is a question I would like to ask you. It is about a promise I made to my mother; to find the name of the all devouring beast that haunts her still."

Fully composed now, Amergin said, "I know, and I shall get to that in my own time."

'Then it is not Thoth?' thought Malceni.

"Correct," continued Amergin, "as Thoth is far worse than the beast he will ride. I shall tell you how the Universe was made and what it has to do with your beast. It is esoteric knowledge and you may probably not understand it."

Using his finger, he etched a series of criss-crossed lines in the air. 'The fields of potentiality,' thought Lutrin.

"Yes. How did you ... ? Don't interrupt. One of the beings that lived before the creation of the universe realised that these fields could make him into a god. He sent his thoughts into thirty-seven of those fields. The result was the creation of time and space as we know it. Matter formed into the earth, because matter is energy vibrating at the frequency of the thought. Thoth entered the world with the intention to rule it. Mithras quickly thought up the Sun to seed good life and mankind on earth. His brothers thought up the Moon to give life to the Finni. And then Mithras combined the Moon and Tree to give all life a soul and bring forth the Picts. The Moon, as I hope you know, is the hidden light that both illuminates the soul and gives life to the nature spirits. Today, humans have already begun to worship nature spirits and the land itself. This is the root of organised belief structures. Some have already moved on from this to Gods and Goddesses. When people realise that they can't appease or dictate to nature, they will try to subdue it. Invoking spirits, sacrifice and worship, only serves to give Thoth more power. Working with nature spirits like Pan, as friends and allies, is the only way to dis-empower Thoth. Organised systems of belief Lutrin; they are what will form the many headed beast."

"But how do we change the original thought pattern?" Asked Lutrin.

"I think," said Aniel, "we chose to incarnate, in order to ultimately answer that question."

"No," screamed Malceni, "No". They all turned to see Malceni looking over the lectern. "I saw myself fall into darkness, and you ... you Lutrin did nothing to save me."

"Fool of a Pict, you no longer trust your friend," said Amergin. This very idea could be the act that brings about what you fear most."

Amergin took the mirror, placed it in a hard protective case and handed it to Lutrin. "You should both leave now. There is nothing more for you here. But remember this, the source of your power lies with the mystery of the Moon-Tree relationship and its relationship to nature. Now go."

"We shall meet again old man. Or should I say, youngest brother of Mithras," said Lutrin.

"Does that make you our Uncle?", asked Malceni.

"Go."

"Amergin," said Aniel, "they can't go just yet. It is late. Picts love a good supper. I also understand that Malceni is on somewhat of a holiday, and it is their birthday. We should all spend the night here, Picts and Finns."

"Of course," replied Amergin. "Please forgive my rudeness," he said, giving Malceni a glance.

"Yes," replied Aniel, "but may we ask you about our earlier predicament?"

"You may ask."

"Well then?"

"Oh, yes. Well, I can't , I mean, shouldn't at the moment. You see, quite clearly some time-lines are being messed around with. But no harm, I think, has been done. Certain events must play themselves out before harmony is restored to the eye of the time-line."

"But," began Malceni.

"It is okay Mal, I understand and, being almost immortal, I am sure that Aniel does too," said Lutrin.

Aniel nodded, "Yes Lutrin, in the wider time-passage what puzzles us now may be the cause of much merriment later."

Amergin clapped his hands and a harpist entered the room. "Meet Garaldina. She will entertain you whilst I see where our supper is."

As Amergin left the room, Malceni stared at Garaldina's long blonde hair; which had been tied at the back with a ribbon. 'She must be the most beautiful human ever,' he thought. He turned away and tried to think of something else. "It is very cold in here," he said, rubbing his hands and stamping his feet, "shall I light a fire?"

"Do not," said Tarquin raising his hand, "I once suggested that, and Amergin became very angry. 'No wael-rec, no wael-rec*',' he said to me."

Garaldina strolled across the room, picked up her lyre, and began to sing 'Lament for a sister'.

* Anglo-Saxon for 'slaughter-smoke'

"What is this drivel?" shouted an angry Amergin on returning from the kitchen. He stared at Garaldina with deep blue eyes.

"I am sorry master. Buy you said that when I met a 'Lutrin' that I should sing this lament."

"Yes, I think I do remember saying that," said Amergin, waving her away. She picked up her lyre and started to hurry out of the room. As she did so, she fell by Lutrin's feet and thrust an object into his hands.

After she had left, they all shared a quiet supper together. Their host said very little and looked very tired. Tarquin told Malceni and Lutrin tales about the ancient Finni warriors in distant lands. He started to sing, but Aniel indicated that he shouldn't when Amergin lowered his head and grunted.

"Where was I?" said Amergin suddenly waking up. "Oh, I have not been a very good host I'm afraid. Let us all retire and dream of a hearty breakfast before you leave in the morning."

Lutrin and Malceni shared a room. At least it was warm there. Someone had kindly lit the fire and laid out fresh straw for them. There was a thick rug in front of the fire, and a little old table with two armchairs. Under orders from the wizard, Garaldina entered with two jugs of ale.

"Shall we?" said Malceni looking at the jugs, "I've never tried it before." Garaldina put the ale on the table and smiled at a blushing Malceni.

Lutrin pulled out his pipe. "It is an old briar of Brude's, he won't miss it."

"I've never tried that either. This is not such a bad birthday after all," gleamed Malceni.

Garaldina indicated that someone was outside, and left quickly.

Lutrin lit the pipe. When they had finished, Malceni poured them both an ale each. They must have drank too quickly, or was it the leaf. Their heads began to spin.

Amergin was about to knock on the door, but when he smelt the leaf's aroma he quickly moved off to his own room, muttering under his breath as he went.

In the middle of the night, Tarquin crept into Malceni and Lutrin's room. "We are leaving now. Quietly. We will rely on you to get us across the lake safely. Can you do it?"

They thought they would feel a little groggy, but their heads were very clear. "Yes, if there is light." As they left they noticed that they had hardly touched a drop of the ale.

They crept down the stairs, along the hallway and reached the front door. As they opened it they heard a wizard's voice behind them, "What is wrong? Guests, leaving like thieves in the night." Amergin put his staff aside, walked forward, and fell on his knees. "I can not say yet. We, I, am not always as I appear. In future, remember me. A friend should always recognise friend." Tears came from his cold grey eyes. At that point the castle creaked, shook, and grew larger. The front door was now a few feet away.

"Ooh", groaned Amergin, "go now, in case you too are affected."

Malceni noticed that Amergin looked a little older than earlier. "Oops," he said, and ran.

It was still very dark outside. They did not speak until they had gone sufficient distance from the castle to feel safe. Aniel and Tarquin looked unchanged, but Lutrin and Malceni had aged a few years.

"Open a bridge, master Lutrin. Now," asked Aniel.

"There is no light," he replied frantically.

"Starlight you shall have," said Tarquin. It was too dark to see, but Tarquin pulled a moonstone from his pocket and held it above the water, "Ilura latha Gilwain. Ilura Latha Gilwain. Quick Lutrin, grab hold of the light from the hidden star of Gilwain."

Lutrin opened a bridge to Eyribol. "Over the top," he said, running onto the bridge.

*

"What did Garaldina give you Lutrin?" asked Tarquin later. Lutrin opened his tunic to reveal a flat clear crystal pendant with an image of Panara inside it.

"It is a beautiful gift. Usually I would be cautious, because you do not know where the gift came from. But somehow, I feel it will bring you good luck."

"I think so too. There are many mysteries here but it could drive us crazy even trying to guess. I am patient enough to let our lives unfold, without chasing riddles," said Lutrin.

"A wise choice I think. Nevertheless, keep your tura open to the answers, or at least to the clues that you come across. The world is changing, I can feel it all around."

"What tongue was that you spoke earlier; it was like nothing I have heard before?" asked Lutrin.

"It was ancient Uralic, as told by the Finni to the Finnic. Well, it is time for us to head home. Goodbye Lutrin and you too Malceni." Malceni nodded.

Aniel and Uriel waved a gesture of goodbye.

*

Back in the castle, after the front door was closed and the guests had left, Amergin stumbled to his feet.

"Come here," commanded a voice from the top of the staircase.

"For pity's sake, give me some rest," said Amergin.

"That was not a request."

Amergin walked slowly up the stairs and stood in front of a tall, full-length mirror. Amergin's cold grey eyes looked into the mirror. Deep blue eyes stared back at him.

"You can not stop me brother. Any further meddling and I will reverse the time compression in this castle and watch you turn to dust."

"Mithras will deal with you Thoth," said Amergin.

"Hah, Mithras, when was the last time he helped you? He is weak."

"He loves you still."

"That is his weakness."

"What do you want?"

"I want to gloat dear brother. Gloat and enjoy your misery as I explain my plans and know that you know that there is nothing you can do about them."

"That is your weakness."

Thoth laughed out, "We shall see. Did you like the 'mystery' package that you – I mean I – had Garaldina pass to Lutrin?" he said sniggering. Amergin said nothing. "Oh go on, ask me what was in it."

"What was in it?" said Amergin.

"A gift. A gift for Lutrin. It was his birthday after all. A gift that will haunt him if he finds out what it really is."

For a moment the blue eyes flashed a tinge of grey as Amergin fought back.

"Your effort weakens you far more than it hurts me. Anyway, the 'gift'. Where do I begin. Yes, that's right, Lutrin made it all possible when he created a paradox in time, you know, when he allowed Panara back into this reality. A trifling paradox really, eventually it would have worked itself out. But, energetically, a paradox nonetheless. As a lord of time I felt it my duty to intervene."

"What black-hearted thing did you do?"

"As I said, my duty. You see, I compressed that paradox into a crystal. Panara is going around and around for eternity. Am I not benevolent little brother, giving out immortality to a simple creature. As for little Lutrin, do you think I should tell him." Amergin winced. "I see not," continued Thoth, "and I agree. I can enjoy the irony even more." Amergin went to leave. "Oh, I have not finished."

"Surely that is enough?" said Amergin.

"I never have my fill."

"Then I would pity you, as a rule."

"That was your weakness wasn't it. Pity. You had your chance long ago and missed it. To resume the story.

The knife, you remember, the knife I gave Taesus. Well it was the fifth knife of Tibias."

"I had guessed. 'Five knives for five brothers', and the fifth is for the youngest."

"Funny eh. Taesus thinks he has the great knife to kill Thoth, when in fact he has the knife that can kill you. Another amusing irony. Very soon, all your friends will think that you are me. They will then kill you. At that point, get it, 'point', your body will rise again with me as it sole occupier."

"And then they will know that I was innocent."

"Oh yes, the truth will out, but think how weakened they will be to find out that they actually killed you, and made me more powerful than ever at the same time."

"Why did you make me give Lutrin the mirror?" asked Amergin, changing the subject.

"That was just a little 'extra'. You and I both know the mirror is useless. But it will teach him to treasure possessions and seek for adventure and change. At the same time it will drive a wedge between him and Malceni. Poor Malceni has greedy tendencies you see. Your pathetic effort to advise them will be little more than a memory."

Amergin grinned in the mirror. Thoth looked a little disturbed. "What have you done?"

"Done," said Amergin, "not done, but undoing. Your undoing. The handle of the mirror that cont..."

"Contains the first knife of Tibias," said Thoth, "the knife that can kill Mithras?"

Amergin was laughing now. "Fool. There is no first knife anymore. From the one knife, four knives were made by Tibias. No knife can kill our brother. No, the hidden mirror handle contains, and always has contained, what you would know as the second knife."

"What?" howled Thoth, as Amergin's laughter almost matched his own tone.

"Yes, the one destined for you," he said, dancing in a circle. The castle creaked and he danced faster. But then he stopped, and noticed that he looked older again. "My despised Thoth. Another weakness you have is underestimating those whom you think are simple, and the simple things they like, like loyalty and friendship. Rest assured, you are in as much danger as I am. The difference is, that I am tired and would gladly go home beyond the fields again, if it means you have to go home too."

Thoth was frightened. "But I can't go back. You know that."

"You can. Mithras has said so."

"Mithras. Mithras the fool. What does he know? I know I will die."

"Yes, your wicked nature would die, but you would return as you once were."

"That is a fate worse than death," said Thoth, "back to being the advisor that always has to say the opposite to a bunch of weaklings. No, I won't go. I won't."

"But those weaklings, as you call us, have all grown up now. Things would be different. Who knows, together we could all create another world?"

Thoth thought about it for a moment, and, for a moment, he gave off a powerful aura. The air was sweet with the fragrance of roses. There was a sound. A frequency. A vibration. The aura felt more powerful and more beautiful than love itself. Amergin was engulfed by the aura. His skin started to tighten. The wrinkles smoothed out. The years fell from him and he stood aghast at the image in the mirror. Still Thoth thought, and then he said kindly, "Remember this night little brother."

"What have you done?" asked Amergin.

"Buying a little favour with the mighty 'M.' You are free to go. Go. Go on. I shall remain here."

"Do you mean the war is over?"

"No. I am who I am whilst I remain in this world. Your appeal to me was not from you, they were the words of Mithras speaking through you. I have listened to the message and acted as best I can."

"Oh please, please let us go home?"

"No," Thoth said angrily, "do not arouse my anger. Already I think I might change my mind. Go, before you regret it."

"I will go, and yes I will remember this night forever."

"Ahh," screamed Thoth, "run, run for your miserable life, I can not live with this goodness in me for much longer. The pain, oh the pain brother. Run. Run before I can resist no more."

Amergin leapt down the stairs and out of the castle. He knew that he had to get off Manni, not just leave the castle, before Thoth changed his mind.

As he ran, he saw Garaldina. "You too," he shouted, grabbing hold of her hand, "and you as well," grabbing a crabby old faery as they went. The faery then grabbed another faery.

As they ran, Amergin pulled a whistle from under his cloak and blew. A few seconds later, they heard the whooshing sound of wings. It was the Roc. Without any further words, all four escapees mounted the Roc, which ascended immediately for the sky. As they did so, they could feel the sickly pull of an energy field. The second faery to be rescued was pulled away from the giant bird and fell back towards Manni.

"Got you," boomed an almighty voice. They could see the face of Thoth closing in on them. The Roc was slowing.

Amergin looked back and uttered the ancient invocation, "Clem shelac mac agal oshanto." A blast of wind rebounded off the energy field and hit the Roc, propelling it away from the boundaries of Manni. They were safe. As Amergin looked back, the face began to fade, but he heard a faint whisper, "Remember me little brother."

During the flight over the great lake, Amergin thought that he could hear Mithras say to him, 'now you know why I can not kill him, now you know.'

'Yes,' thought Amergin, 'I know. But does it change anything?' Silently they flew, until the Roc rested on the peak of the Shivering Mountain. Amergin needed time to recuperate.

***

Chapter 5: **MEARE MAGIC**

Three years after the incident on Manni, Brude called Lutrin and Malceni together. A group of Taezali were going to the great meeting at Athelney. Groups within the Taezali knew about other people from beyond Sunna, because once every forty years the Finns brought together a few members of different races to a place about one hundred and fourteen miles South-East of Eyribol.

A Finnic escort had arrived. There was much excitement in the camp and those chosen to go felt happy to be a part of such a rare event. Malceni could hardly believe his luck at being permitted to go with Lutrin. In fact, this reflected more about how Malceni felt about himself than about how others treated him. Ever since his birth he had been treated as a son by Brude and Volas.

Brude ordered a detour to Deedle's mountain; where many tons of Blue-John had been loaded onto donkey-laden carts. The carts were guarded by a group of battle-ready Gridolers.

Much of the land governed by the Gridolers was uninhabited. The scenery was breathtaking, but the weather could be harsh. There were plenty of wolves around, who were friendly enough, and a few bears, who very much kept themselves to themselves. The Gridolers had a good relationship with the wolves. On hunting days, they inadvertently hunted together. The wolves would track the deer or wild-boars, followed by the Gridolers who killed it and kept the tastiest bits, and then the wolves would eat what the Gridolers left. Tilli was trying to learn their language, but, as yet, he only knew a few words.

After many days of travel, Aniel announced that they would arrive by tomorrow afternoon. It was windy, and rain was heading towards them. Fortunately, they would soon arrive at a Gorge; where they would spend the night in the caves. A few Finns went on ahead, shouting, "Eteen! Eteen!" to Malceni.

Tarquin passed Uriel. "They are calling you forward, to the front, would you like to join us Malceni?" he asked.

"Sure, yes, thank you. Are you coming Lu?"

"Lutrin and I must discuss a few things," said Uriel, "we will catch up with you later."

After they had moved off, Lutrin turned to Uriel, "What was all that about?"

"Brude said Malceni could do with a trip, without you."

"Why have they gone on ahead?"

"The Gorge is home to bears." Lutrin looked a little shocked. "Do not be concerned for his safety. He will think he is in danger, but he won't be really. My people will be asking the head of the Bear Clan for permission to sleep in their caves. If she agrees, we will charm the other bears and send them into a deep sleep tonight."

That night their spirits were high. With a wall of rock behind them and the rain now ahead of them, they lit many fires and prepared a supper of fresh water 'Kala'. Although the food was communally served, lots of different groups gathered together near the fires. Brude was way over the other side of the camp, so Lutrin and Malceni pulled out their pipes and began discussing his encounter with the bears. Shortly after they had lit them, Brude appeared.

"You are both twenty-one now, so I will say no more about the fact that you look like seasoned puffers, rather than novices." Brude sat next to them and poured them a pint of ale each. "I can think of no better time for a Seeder to have his first drink with his sons." Malceni found it difficult to hold back the tear from his eye. Brude patted his head. "I should have expressed that feeling sooner. I have always loved you as a son. I couldn't bring myself to say it, because...because...I was afraid that I might lose you. What if your mother came back for you? And then I felt guilty because a part of me hoped that she never would."

It went quiet, so, almost pretending that nothing had just happened, they talked about other things instead; including Lutrin's confession about the incident with Panara five years earlier. Nevertheless, a word spoken can not be taken back, and the three of them went to bed very happy indeed.

*

When they finally arrived at their destination, they saw that the Finns had done them proud. Huts had been built high into the trees. There was heating and an object the Picts had not seen before, something Tarquin called 'a mattress'. After an afternoon nap, Lutrin approached Brude, 'Father, why are we here.'

"Lu, I am old. This will be my last such meeting. I think I might be the last head carer of an undivided Pictland. Picts should not have egos but I would like to know what this new land will look like one day. Your mother said that it may have something to do with you. I have told the Finns this and they believed it also. You are their guest of honour. Go with your friends and help them to assist you in this evening's storytelling."

*

Lutrin sat behind a grassy knoll, close to the road they had travelled along, overlooking a small lake and woodland. At times, the local faeries would whisper in his ear. Most of what they said he listened to intently because he was concerned with his lack of preparation for an event such as this.

He then spent quite some time on his own trying to at least master some elements within his mirror. He had quickly learnt that if he did not gaze at something he no longer wanted to see, then the image would change to something else. He asked Malceni to help him, and also to make sure that nobody was watching. On occasions he noticed that Malceni was staring into the mirror over his shoulder. "Mal, I have told you that I will teach you when you are more mature, and also when I have mastered it as well as I can myself. Just look how you linger at a horrible picture, whereas I am looking for beauty."

"I know. It is just that I need to know what happened."

Lutrin was too busy now for this discussion again. "You are always so gloomy. I've promised you, haven't I?" and said no more.

*

Later that evening Lutrin began his tale. He didn't know it at the time, but it would be a tale passed on for many generations. This is because the devas and faeries present intended to put on quite a show. It was agreed with Lutrin beforehand that everything he said tonight would be played out in front of the audience, and, in some cases, fragments of the show would be left permanently within the land.

"The Meare by twilight is a wondrous and majestic sight," he said. "The trees and rocks surrounding the pool stand as monuments to an age long forgotten in the outside world." At this point the atmosphere became ionised. They could feel power and wisdom oozing from the land as the blue and green water lapped gently against the shore.

Lutrin felt he was starting to narrate a piece of history rather than tell a story. He wasn't sure of the energy he was experiencing, but decided to go with the flow and continue channeling.

"The lush meadow grass begins its dance, as the gentle breeze passes by on the endless voyage it must continue until the world's end. From the sky, atmospheric changes in the cosmos cause cascading showers of light to rain upon the land." The colours of the rainbow floated in the air, revealing faery dancers performing their own brand of spellbinding, often sensuous ritual of thanks to the forces of nature.

"At times like this, humans may be unable to resist the aura emanating from the faery people and follow the dancers back into realms that they may never leave. The Tor of Meare is also in Athelney, albeit in another dimension. A ruined church tower however, is all that may be physically seen there." 'How far ahead am I looking?' he thought, and remembered that the audience would have heard that too.

He heard Brude's words softly on his tura, 'concentrate my son, or you will lose the magic.'

'What's a Church?' thought Malceni.

"Shush Mal."

"Humph!"

Lutrin had to make-up the next line, a storyteller's poetic licence, to return him back onto his track, "Instead of a ruined church tower there stands a fine castle."

On the hilltop, near where they sat, a huge building shimmered into sight – 'this was real magic', he thought, 'my friends are working hard to create this image.'

"As you can see there is no portcullis or similar trappings like those of a fortress because no enemies can enter Athelney. Instead there is a huge oak door with Lions' heads embossed onto the wood. A festival is about to begin in this castle, which has not been inhabited for generations, but nevertheless is in perfection condition. And, as it is only a tiny castle it is warm and cosy with fine silken tapestries and softly woven rugs." Lutrin indicated that they should enter the castle. The audience could see all of these things in front of their eyes.

Lutrin realised that the storytelling, narrating, and creation of images had personally brought the audience into the story. At this point, the faeries took on a larger form and began to dance and play music. It was very rare for a faery to do this and they looked in appearance like the Elfin. Everyone was awe-struck at the faeries ability to turn their spiritual perception of love and nature into sounds and music.

To 'ground' those present, Lutrin returned to the narrative, "Mystical and ethereal rivulets of cascading ancient sounds came alive within the listeners souls, causing their minds to evoke scenes from another dimension. The unicorns listened to the music as if they had heard it before. This music was from the age long gone when all dimensions existed side by side in a world of peace and beauty".

At the edge of the gathering, two unicorns appeared in their midst; their tears falling to the ground. He did not notice, because he was too busy too notice, that they stared all the time at Lutrin's pendant. The presence of the unicorns was not planned.

It was the Finns turn to gasp, for now the storytelling turned to channeling ancient knowledge.

"When mankind became religious he became discontented with nature. They made enemies of the animals and slaughtered the unicorns because they were jealous of the spiritual entities who had magical powers whilst they had none. The entities fled to another dimension vowing not to be reconciled with humans again."

Thankfully, the mood turned back to its original course. "The lively rhythm and magical moods of this music was seductive and entrancing; occasionally provocative. The listeners were transformed by the spell-enchanting and captivating passion of the faeries radiant and visionary melodies that fascinated their senses and rippled through their imagination with a disarming tenderness of pure enchantment and inspiration."

Long after the faery music stopped, the audience stayed silent as they continued to seemingly float in a world without trouble, the old world was here at least for a short while.

Lutrin continued with the story, "In the distance one of the celestial guardians of Meare had been listening to the radiant tranquility of the faeries legendary transforming music. They were kindred spirits, him and them, and in the stillness of his angelic sleep he felt the emergence of their natural magic from another sky.

He was pleased that the humans he guarded had welcomed their initiation to the faeries pathways of love with a reverence so deep that for the first time since those old days he played his healing lyre to complement his soul mates in Athelney."

Once again, the unexpected overtook events. The audience had only just got over the entities' music when they felt the calling from the guardians' lyre to let them be the keeper of their dreams. His precious love for them took them to the edge of their dreams and beyond. All of those present felt their hearts expand, felt almost a giddiness, and a heartfelt belief that this was the start of a new age of love.

*

Brude was the first to congratulate his son. "That was a fine story Lu, and to think that your mother was once worried that you might lose your tura. Never in my life have I seen such magic in a story."

"That was the faeries" replied Lutrin.

"No, that is what you thought was going to happen. They provided the music of course, but it was a powerful projection of your tura that created many of the images," continued Brude.

"It was not just 'projection,' as you say." They turned to see Aniel walking towards them quite seriously.

"You were permitting scenes from the past and future to become part of the present for a moment in this time. Not even Finns can sustain all three. I ask you Lutrin the Lucid, son of Brude, son of Bred, are you a lord of time like Amergin?"

"No. At least I do not think so."

"Maybe", continued Aniel, " but there is more to this Pict than meets the eye. We should talk more Brude, about the image concerning the slaughter of magical creatures. I know this has happened before, but the manner in which Lutrin spoke suggests a peril much closer. Anyway, tomorrow will do. The night is still young. We have many poems and songs to hear before sleep, and of course much ale and food for some. Well done Lutrin, I shall follow your development with much interest."

After Brude and Aniel walked towards the main gathering a tall dark-haired handsome man stepped out from behind a tree not ten paces from where Lutrin stood. "Good evening Master Pict. I hope I didn't startle you."

"I did not notice you there, a rare thing to hide from one of the Finni folk and two Picts," 'but you did not startle me.'

The round-faced blue-eyed man laughed.

"My name is Taesus from Dogger, or rather that's what my people have called me since my youth." Taesus was dressed in a design similar to Tarquin, but the colours were darker and the fabric was only cloth.

"I presume that is because of your long mane of hair with the ribbon tied to it," said Malceni, appearing suddenly from behind Taesus.

Taesus span around with his knife in his hand, but Malceni was on him fast. Standing between Lutrin and Taesus, now stood Malceni with Taesus' knife in his hand.

"Your understanding of our names does you credit little Pict, but your manners do not."

'He was spying on you Lutrin.'

"Speak out Mal. He can hear our thoughts too."

"He was listening to your conversation earlier, and he knows about the mirror. What do you say to that nosy?"

"Return my knife and we will speak as comrades. If not, then you will see how a human fares in hand-to-hand combat."

Lutrin stepped forward, "Neither of you will fight in this special place." He took the knife from Malceni and placed it at his own feet. "Weapons were not supposed to be brought into the gathering. Now please answer my friend."

"I didn't trust that Aniel. He was a rebel, did you know that? I heard that he once spilt Finni blood and that Aniel isn't even his real name."

"Like yours is not Taesus." Lutrin paused and thought for a moment. "Aniel means 'virtue,' so he took that name as a reminder to himself. Whatever helps people, who change their names, to live better lives, is surely a good thing. I am also aware of something he is not. He is not looking for a way home, because he thinks he is beyond redemption. I know that he is not."

Taesus walked forward and gestured towards his knife. Lutrin nodded.

"Is it the mirror that gives you this knowledge?" asked Malceni.

"No. I am not sure that it was the mirror which revealed it to me. Being here in this place makes me feel more, more ... ."

"Powerful?", suggested Taesus.

"No", continued Lutrin, "I was thinking ... feel more like myself, who I am, what I am meant to be."

"Where did you get the knife?" said Malceni. "It seems familiar."

"Some years ago I was given the knife by Amergin. He said it was made by an evil god before the World began. The knife can kill Thoth, which is why he left it beyond the Universe. But the wizard said that he brought the knife with him."

"I thought that Amergin doesn't leave Manni anymore."

"Let me see the knife again," asked Lutrin. He beckoned them to sit down behind the tree and took out the mirror to compare their craftsmanship.

"I must admit," said Malceni, "they do have similar designs on them, and a familiar 'feel' to them."

Taesus became cheerful. "Let's go and celebrate a new friendship. If Malceni will permit it that is?"

'I do,' thought Malceni smiling, "but only if you will sing us a song later about Dogger."

"Yes. That I will. Yes." The three of them stood up and headed for the main gathering.

Malceni had been asking Taesus many questions, about how humans communicate with one another, until finally he said, "Taesus, do humans feel lonely?"

"At times, yes, but mostly when we are so wrapped up in our own thoughts that we fail to see the love and beauty being offered to us. Life should never be dull. A man and woman can share a lifetime together and still not know as much as a Pictish couple in their first year of bonding."

"It is true that Picts see everything another Pict does. We do not have compartments in our trees, as walls would be meaningless anyway. I do not think though, that it is as romantic as you make it sound. But then again, I am not bonded. Picts like Lutrin and I have no partners. We are not seen as proper Picts you see. And, in the 'different' group we belong to, we are not permitted to bond with one another because of the close family ties. Although we came from different tribes, we were all the offspring of Taezali's who had moved elsewhere."

"I'm sorry, I didn't know this."

"It will be okay, I think. See Lu over there." Malceni pointed to a group of small Elfin sitting close to Lutrin. Taesus and Malceni exchanged grins.

"His wisdom goes way beyond his years," said Taesus.

"I agree. You see, the small Elfin are in the same position as us. Forbidden to bond."

"An alliance of Pict and Elf. It was no chance that this meeting took place I think. See, Brude and Aniel are looking at them also." Malceni nodded. "Earlier, I saw you teasing that tiny Elf over there", continued Taesus, "a little unkind don't you think, to mock a person with a lisp?"

"I was not," he replied, defending himself, "It was her size I was being silly about."

"You wish you hadn't done it now. You like her?"

"Yes, but I don't know how to turn it around. When I am the one doing the teasing she enjoys it, but she may never see me as anything but a friend. She can't bare anyone else mocking her size."

"Such is life. But don't wait too long, for her to see otherwise, or for you to choose someone else. I have a feeling that many of your kind are choosing tonight."

"What?"

"Do not underestimate your turas. I am telepathic, and that ability speeds up many choices I might take, how much more a tura?"

They watched as Lutrin and Aniel's daughter, Lucknow, left the crowd and went for a walk. The avenues of trees were lit by torches, so, in order to get some privacy from Finnic eyes and Pictish turas, they left the path briefly to share thoughts in the woods. At one point when they were sharing their time together, Lutrin felt a presence nearby. He lifted his arm over them both and activated his magical ability to match in with his environment and remain unseen.

*

On his return from the woods, Lutrin collected three mugs of wine and went to sit beside Malceni and Taesus. Taesus was grinning. "Here, try this," said Lutrin. "It is made from fermented grapes. It is as good as the beer they make from 'hops.' What a blessed land this is."

"But the heather ale that Brude brought is even better," said Taesus.

"But would you say that if that was all you could drink? Choice my friend. I want choice. And if I stay in the Gap I certainly will not have that. There is more to life."

He stopped and looked back towards Lucknow.

'This wine was not the only fermentation taking place this evening I think,' thought Malceni.

Aniel waved a signal to Taesus, who realised that it was his turn to sing. "Well gentlemen, you shall now hear a Dogger man sing an old drinking song. However, in light of what we have discussed, I have changed the words somewhat." He stood up and waited for silence.

Whilst Lutrin had a moment alone with Malceni he said, "He has met Amergin Mal. We both met him on the same day when we were teenagers. But surely he must remember me. I did save his life after all!"

Taesus began to sing a song that would one day be called, **'The Song of Picton.'**

"If you could see, what I can see
Much better 'twould be.
If I could see, what you can see,
This World would be.

For we are men, that live alone,
Inside our own heads,
With demons there, together we
Lonely paths we tread.

Now he can see, what she can see,
All of the time.
And she can see, what he can see,
In their own minds.

But you are Picts, your turas shared,
So act merrily.
All your lives, together these,
Shared in harmony.

Now we have seen, what we have seen,
What a joy to behold
Elf and Pict, together you,
Good lives are sowed.

For we are all, Tibias seed,
Sharing our kin.
That knowledge now, lightens the load,
For all those herein."

"Enough," demanded Aniel. "Certain tidings, that may or may not come to pass, should not be first revealed in a drunkards song. Especially as what you sing about does not have my full blessing yet."

Brude was furious with Aniel but, before he could speak, Lutrin said, "The decision is not yours to make."

"I say it is so, because your father already wants this alliance. Therefore, it is I who must give final blessing."

Lucknow walked over to Lutrin and took his hand in hers. "What may happen is neither yours nor Brude's decision. It is ours to make," she said.

Brude was actually pleased to see Lutrin and Lucknow's reaction. "A right pair of rascals we have reared Aniel."

"You mistook what Lucknow said father. When she said 'ours,' she literally meant ..." he paused to wave a hand across the group of young people now standing behind Brude and Aniel, " ... ours. Our people."

"Father," said Lucknow, "could any ship bare an Elf from Portowest?"

Tears welled up in his eyes. "I truly do not know."

"Precisely," she said, "as it is our doom to stay here then we intend to be happy."

Lutrin decided to calm the situation some what. "Although we have stated our intentions a little earlier than we intended to, nothing more need be said for now."

"As he says," said Brude, "I suggest we all have some sleep. If you recall, Aniel, we have many discussions tomorrow."

After many of the gathering went to their tree huts, Lutrin turned to Taesus and asked him directly about that day on the beach all those years ago. Taesus was taken aback.

"But Lutrin, I swear that I have no memory of you that day. It was Amergin who rescued me and then, a few minutes later, gave me the knife."

"Perhaps Amergin altered your memory."

"Perhaps," said Taesus, "but why?"

"I think there may be a way of finding out at least part of the puzzle. Give me the mirror for a moment," said Malceni thoughtfully.

"We have been through this so many times," replied Lutrin wearily.

"But I have an idea. Listen. You see pleasant images. I see unpleasant ones. If we combine out turas, and create a balance, then Taesus can also look into the mirror. The three of us should look together."

"I'm game," said Taesus, "what harm can be done?"

Lutrin looked troubled. "None, unless we misread what we see. However, I agree."

Although Lutrin had not used the mirror to see reverse time-lines before, the process seemed similar. After a murky start, Amergin came abruptly into view.

"So, this is the poika?" said an enormous, both in height and width, bald and rough-looking battle-scarred warrior.

He was talking to, to ... ah yes ... one of the Finns!

"Yes. This is Lu-trin," replied Aniel, who was actually standing next to Taesus and not Lutrin.

"I've never seen a Pict before. He looks human."

"As you said Norbold," said Amergin, "You have not seen a Pict before."

Norbold continued, "Our Shaman knew that a powerful child had been born to the Picts. One that could destroy us, or make us Lords of all."

"Shamans, like wizards, often overstate things Norbold," said Aniel, "he will prove worthy enough for the Orci."

"We shall see."

"The poika must take his knife," continued Amergin.

"That was not mentioned before."

Aniel too, looked as puzzled as Norbold.

"It is important to his abilities. It helps him to concentrate."

"He will have to learn to concentrate without it," finished Norbold, who led Taesus down the beach and into a long-boat not far from three others that lay off-shore. At that point a shout was heard from above. A small group of Finns quickly ran down the path to the beach. Ignoring Aniel, but acknowledging Amergin, they started firing arrows at the boats. Taesus turned, to see a rock land on Amergin's head and a startled Aniel take up a position behind the Finns. Lutrin and Panara appeared and made their way to the beach and helped Amergin to his feet.

"Betrayal. Attack. Back-stabber," shouted Norbold, who aimed a large spear at Amergin. Seeing the gesture, Amergin darted behind Panara. Moments later, she was dead. Meanwhile, Aniel must have made his way back up the path.

Lutrin, Malceni and Taesus looked up at each other and the image was gone.

"Well," said Malceni, "I once said he was crafty, in a mischievous sort of way. But this is pure wickedness, I think."

"What do you mean, 'think'?" snorted Taesus.

"They must have been protecting Lutrin you see."

"No," said Lutrin, "That does not make it right. All sacrifice is wrong, especially one that is forced upon the innocent. The man-price it too high."

They heard a rustling of leaves nearby. Malceni was out like a bolt. "Got him. Oh, it's you," he said as he sent Aniel sprawling forward into the light.

"It is ill fitting for a lord of your rank to sneak on peoples' private doings," said Lutrin.

"You three know as much about that as anyone," Aniel said defensively.

"Explain yourself, please," said Lutrin.

"I do not talk about past deeds or errors. What I will say is this. I never attempted to hand Taesus over to Norbold."

"But we all ...," said Taesus.

"No you did not," said Aniel, "you were sharing thoughts, so loudly that you've kept many of us awake. Not just each others thoughts, but also thoughts that float on the ether, waiting like vampires to intrude upon a time-line."

"What is he going on about?" sneered Malceni.

"When we 'think'," continued Aniel, "it creates an energy which, under the right circumstances, can enter this reality. The best example is one directly related to your Shamanic journey with the mirror tonight." He sighed, and then poured himself some mead. The others filled their tankards as well. "I did, once, think of handing Taesus over."

"There, told you so," said Malceni spilling a little beer down his tunic.

"Shush," chorused Taesus and Lutrin.

"I said this during a meeting with Amergin on Manni. He had said that he wanted to hand Lutrin over to Norbold, as the man-price for peace. My first thought is what you saw tonight. In reality I dismissed the idea almost as quickly as I had first voiced it." Looking for intellectual support, he turned to Taesus. "You must have seen similar things with the Dogger psychics?"

"Perhaps. I had to learn how to use my gift. I would hear all kinds of thoughts and believe them all. So I asked a good psychic for an opinion. She said that everything I'd hear was indeed 'truth,'; but they were only 'passing truths' because they were only fleeting thoughts that the other people had. I concluded that a major problem people have is what is the right amount of energy to give any given 'thought.' Should thoughts be given any energy?"

"But what if it is a good thought?" questioned Lutrin, "like the hope I discussed earlier."

"I suspect that no time should be given to 'thought' because you will only suffer later."

"Do you mean, if I desire something and do not get it, then I will suffer?" asked Malceni thinking about the mirror.

"Yes, and no. It is much deeper that that. You see, what is the point of thinking anything other than what already is. Many 'wise men' talk about 'desire' equaling 'suffering.' But it is not so. 'Thought,' not desire, is the root of all suffering. Desire may cause individual suffering for someone interested in their own spirituality. But 'thought' is the cause of suffering for all people."

Taesus barely noticed that Lutrin was shaking him, or that the left hand of Aniel was on his head.

"Come Taesus," Aniel commanded, "No more channeling."

Taesus snapped out of it. "Wow. That felt good," he said, "I feel great. Ask me something. Go on, anything."

"I hope you believe me gentlemen," said Aniel.

"It is true. It is true," said Taesus, "let me say one last thing." The others nodded. "We are all already enlightened. Nothing more needs to be learnt. We chose to be born in this world of illusion. We have all the answers within."

"But don't some people look within to find answers to many things?" asked Aniel.

"Yes. But why bother? Don't you see. Enlightenment and spirituality are the same thing. Just live your life according to how you want to live it. Experience your own sovereignty and allow others to do likewise. A few moments ago I had all knowledge at my fingertips. Now, the only thing I can remember is, 'knowing everything doesn't matter.' Knowledge leads to manipulative power, not enlightenment."

"One last thing Lutrin," continued Aniel, "when I spoke of Taesus with Amergin he had a mirror with him. A mirror very similar to the one which he gave to you."

"What are you suggesting?" Malceni asked Aniel, who started to leave.

"Nothing. No-thing at all. It is time for bed. Good night."

"Did you understand all that Mal?" Lutrin asked a perplexed looking Malceni.

"What? Oh, yes. Hmm, but what do you think a 'vampire' is?"

*

Aniel truly smiled as heard the happy trio laughing. His smile turned to a frown when a vision came to him. It was Lutrin and Lucknow walking hand-in-hand in the woods. Looking up at the Moon, Aniel realised he was looking a few hours into the past.

'Lucknow, I love you,' thought Lutrin.

"And I love you too," she said, "but my father ..."

'Aniel loves you very much. He would die for you.'

"You see all that?" she said.

'Aniel's heart is good. Better than he knows – but do not tell him I said so,' smiled Lutrin.

'I feel that we are being watched,' thought Lutrin, who curved his arm around them both and over his head. The result was that of a 'curtain' enveloping them.

Aniel believed that Lutrin actually existed, in reality, in a number of time-passages. Lutrin, even in a past memory, could interact and change the ending. This was the real reason Brude called him Lutrin the Lucid. Lutrin could change certain things in the past if he didn't like them. That meant that he could, when needed, change time. 'Why doesn't Lutrin know this himself?' Pondered Aniel.

As he was thinking this, he found himself standing outside of time and space. A mist shrouded his sight. A shape, no, a familiar figure, one he felt he knew from long ago, stepped forward ... revealing itself hazily.

The shadow had a message for him, 'Please. Do not go there my friend. Do not delve too far, if you have love in you. I chose this path for the good of the world and because I needed a rest. Yes, a rest. A mortal life, for a while anyway, is what is good for me also. Hold this secret fast to yourself and your redemption is at hand.'

"Hnaef? No. No. It can not be," Aniel cried out. "Only. Only my ... only my accuser can give me forgiveness. Surely you have not been released from the place of waiting yet. None of us return so soon."

'Finn. I asked you not to delve, not for my sake but your own. This final message I confirm. Helping him is helping me. Helping me, helps you. Do not think, only 'be' and remember 'I am'. Aniel knew there was a way home now.

At the meeting the following morning Aniel was in good spirits, as were most of the gatherers. However, the business at hand was not pleasant. Aniel concentrated hard, and a shape, like that of a bear covered with mud, moss and sticks, manifested, then appeared to float forward. Although it had physically moved, nobody could remember it having been stood anywhere else other than where it stood now.

"If you will Brude," said Aniel.

"Yes of course, you will need me to interpret for you." He bowed low to the creature. My friends, continued Brude, "this is the Woodwose of Tajem. He is a unique being that lives in the Tajem forest."

Woodwose spoke quickly and sweetly, but with a bitter guttural sound at the end of each sentence. After a series of whoops and the occasional cough from Brude, their exchange seemed at an end.

"Well", said Brude, "he has informed me that the Orci have been assembling outside our borders. It appears they are looking for a weak spot in the Tajem perimeter. He is concerned that they may burn their way through if they can't find a way. For the benefit of those new to the strengths of the Tajem, let me tell you that a Tajem does not easily burn. Even when it does so, it only smolders for a long time. As such, there is no danger of the Orci's imminent arrival. However, when a Tajem starts to burn it can not be put out. They also take a long time to grow again."

"Why don't you open up a small section and allow them entry?" said Taesus.

"A good idea," echoed the men present.

The Woodwose wasn't pleased, and conveyed his displeasure to Brude.

"He is right," said Brude, "The Tajem is serving the purpose that he first created it for. The Woodwose has spoken. The Tajem is his and all here must respect his sovereignty."

"Moving on then," said Aniel, "last night we heard about the mystical creatures of old. It ties in with some news that has come to my attention. Mithras appeared to me in a dream and warned me that Thoth is plotting some dreadful scheme. He has noticed that no magical or mystical creature has any concept of structured beliefs. As many of you are aware, Gridolers, Finns and Picts do not aspire to such concepts either. Only Man wants its yoke."

"But what has their ignorance to do with any impending devastation?" asked Taesus.

Aniel continued, "Because Thoth wants us all dead. He wants the world to be dominated by men, for he can easily dominate them. In the past he was content to let the earlier races fade, as is the way of all things. But he now fears us; fears that we may find a way to kill him. He can no longer rely on men to kill us because many men are decent. So, he is considering sending a great flood. Of course some of us will survive, but he does not fear the few who will be left. He can then call on the Orci to finish his work for him."

"And what of my people?" enquired Taesus.

"Thoth will not want to hurt you directly. He intends to speed up what would have occurred naturally. Have you not noticed the rising sea levels across the whole of Dogger?"

"Of course we have. Especially as the sea-river along the eastern shore is slowing down and may one day be navigable."

"Thoth will show you some warning first. But then he will unleash his wrath upon this Island. The Dogger people will just get caught up in the troubles, with their land being lost forever. After the flood, much of the Island will return, but not Dogger. I asked you here Taesus, so that you could warn them to come and live on the high ground in Belevedon."

"I will try," said Taesus, "but I doubt that they will believe you. They will say we have been here for centuries and will remain for centuries to come."

"I see Deedle sent some of his kin," mused Aniel, "at least they can carry him tidings of this meeting."

"No," said Brude, "they have other business here. I shall tell Deedle on my way back to Sunna. Volas also had a vision. You may as well know that in my absence the Picts have been told to find refuge as far inland as possible. They are hindered of course by the need for fresh water and fish. Life must go on. Picts like Lutrin are being removed from the Gap also, so they must find shelter elsewhere."

"Brude, I would like you to take Lucknow and her kind back to Sunna with you. Choose high ground and look after them."

"I would be honoured. They will be most welcome."

"There is something I would like to say," said Lutrin. "After listening to Aniel's information about Thoth, I must agree with the Woodwose. Albeit for different reasons.

Thoth will want the Orci to survive completely intact. Therefore, any natural disaster will not affect the northern province. This means that it must be both of the great ice-caps that are being targeted."

Sitting quietly all this time was Malceni. They all turned to look at him as he pulled a cake from his pocket. "Food for thought," he commented, smiling.

The gathering was at an end so they all made ready to go home. Brude had agreed generous terms with the Gridoler host which was guarding the Blue-John. They were delighted and joked that they hoped their task would be a long one.

Brude had allocated each Gridoler a small amount of stone each full Moon. Obviously, there was so much stone that Lutrin would want for nothing when he came to live near Athelney. Lutrin had no idea what the shipment was and didn't ask Brude about it. 'Even a King should have secrets from his poika if he wants to,' thought Lutrin moodily. He paused, and then realised suddenly that Pan had not appeared during the trip with the Finns. 'Busy elsewhere I suppose,' he thought.

The journey back to Sunna was an enjoyable, if uneventful one.

Chapter 6: **DREAMTIME**

On arrival in the South-West of Sunna, the large group of Elfin, and Picts who were like Lutrin, set about creating a 'temporary' village. They decided to construct a mixture of traditional Pictish tree houses and Finnic tree-huts. Generally, the males of either race lived in the tree houses and the females lived just above them in the huts. Lutrin and Lucknow however, had tree houses adjacent to one another.

Many of the other tribes had made long journeys, both to share out food and belongings, and also to see some of their fostered off-spring who were now more readily accepted by all Picts.

'Shame on you,' thought Malceni, 'it is too late now.'

"Forgive them Malceni," said Lutrin, knowing how even more painful it was for Malceni.

"I do Lu. I just wish things had been different."

** **

Winter was fast approaching, and Lutrin had been spending more time practicing looking into different worlds at different times, than using his mirror. 'What use is the mirror,' he pondered, 'when I can actually visit and interact with other places?'

Overhearing Lutrin, Pan came and sat next to him. "I think its time for me to tell you a few things Lutrin. I had hoped Brude or Volas would have done so by now."

"Go on."

"It is about the mirror," he paused to take a breath, "there is nothing special about it at all."

"But what about all the things I have seen with it?"

"Have you noticed that all the older Picts have mirrors?"

"I suppose I had not."

"Well. A conscious decision was made, by all the tribes, not to provide the new race of children with mirrors. They feared your power." Lutrin said nothing, so Pan continued, "Have you noticed that on many of the old stone carvings made by your ancestors that there is usually a picture of a beast, a drawing of the Gap, a centaur and a mirror."

"I presumed that it was a beast that once existed."

"You now know that it was a warning, something foretold long ago."

"Yes. The coming of the many headed beast," said Lutrin.

Pan nodded. "Moving on. The symbol of the Gap." Pan etched the picture on the ground with a stick. The symbol was shaped like two eggs with a narrow bridge between the two. "Did you notice anything similar in Belevedon?"

"Yes. I saw a carving in wood where the two egg-shapes were joined, but without a bridge."

Pan looked sad, "That is an image that men will use. They do not realise that they are foretelling the disappearance of the Gap."

"That is horrible," said Lutrin. "You mean, they will have no conscious choices as to where they want to go to after each mortal life has ended?"

"Precisely," said Pan. "Human made rules will govern where and what they become in their next life. Eventually, even the most wise will believe in this concept."

"So, no more lives as a faery or a tree or a stone?"

"For some, they will only become another living creature that exists in their current reality, and not by choice. For others, they will be trapped in an eternal place of servitude to a God of their own creation."

Lutrin was becoming very disturbed. "We must remind them of the truth."

'What is truth?' thought Pan smiling, "That is what the Picts rock carvings are for. The problem is that nobody will be around to interpret the signs for them. It is very sad. My hope is that one day, when all seems lost, a little voice in the wilderness will sow the seeds of truth." He seemed to be dreaming, and then shook his head. "As to the Centaur," he said, "this is an important reminder about the mythical elements in life."

"Because myths transcend time and space?" said Lutrin.

"Correct."

"And now we finally come to the mirror."

"Hmm," said Pan, "this is a little harder to explain. It is my view that people will think that the mirror is to do with magic. That being the case, they may dismiss all the other signs. I will explain in a moment. The mirror is not magical; the mirror is a reflection of the Picts' tura. All those images you saw, future events you see, and such like, were really created by you."

"I suspected as much that night in Athelney when I met Taesus. What I do not understand though, is why leave this picture behind for future people to see?"

Pan seemed quite pleased with himself now, for this was a secret that he had longed to share with Lutrin. "In those turaless days ahead, the mirror can become a form of tura for all people. Yes, it is but a shadow of a Picts' tura, nevertheless, people could develop a third eye. Afterwards, their minds would be able travel within their light bodies to real places and times."

"A third eye", laughed Lutrin, "and a body made of light."

"We'll deal with the light body later. As for the third eye. I don't mean like the eyes that stick out of your face. I refer to an inner-eye that can be strengthened and built up like any muscle. It will be hard for them and few will believe."

"And that is because of magic?"

"Yes," said Pan. "You see, Thoth is trying to close off the magical realms. He can't destroy them, but he can try and seal them off from this reality. And so, there will come a time when people will have never seen any magic. Oh they will have heard stories about it, but they will say that it is only for the imagination of children. This is one of Thoth's main weapons; as more time passes, people will lose their imagination." An upsurge of pain entered Lutrin. Words stuck in his throat. Tears welled in his eyes, and so too Pan's. "Even children Lutrin. Children will lose their imagination."

"And then Thoth will have won?"

Pan nodded. "I dread to imagine what the world will be like without imagination." He shuddered. "The frightening part is that it will seem to happen in a single generation. The seed of doubt will grow strong over hundreds, thousands of years, there will be no hurry, no impatience, and then 'bang!' Its dark flower will suddenly bloom! The children will be unable to pict-tura anything in their heads. Some adults, the last of their kind, will feel anguish at the terrible loss and call it a grave sin. They will be ignored by people who pat themselves on the back and say 'Are we not civilised now, we who live by logic and reason?' In doing so they will become ensnared by Thoth's shadow."

"You said some people would say what happened was a 'sin.' What is a 'sin' Pan?"

" Sin is an idea created by men in order to control other men and women. Imposing guilt on the innocent, weakens people and makes them more subservient to those who say that they alone can understand good and evil."

Lutrin clearly could not understand, so Pan continued, "People will be told that sin is a reflection of an evil nature. This is utter nonsense. The nature of most intelligent beings is that they are neither good nor evil. Certain spirits or entities may be good or evil but people are not. An evil being, or a good one, has no choice or freewill. They just follow their nature. Take me for example. I will one day be despised when people realise that I don't actually have a soul." Lutrin was shocked. "No, do not be sad," continued Pan, "I am a spirit only. A spirit that will protect nature. Why, if I thought that people would destroy nature then, because I act as a mirror, I will eventually destroy them. I am what I am. Anyway, you have both a spirit and a soul."

"What are they exactly?" asked Lutrin.

"The spirit is a part of how you live; it determines your nature in this life. However, your soul is that immortal part of yourself that you take with you into your next life. Deep within all the atoms that make up your physical form is a particle which travels at the speed of light; this is your light body. However, deeper still, is a particle that travels faster than light until time stands still; this is your soul. You Lutrin, have the rare ability of being able to take your physical body with you to places that your 'light body' can travel to. You are not alone in this."

"And what about the immortal Finns?"

"Oh, although they are Finns, they can still be killed, but they too are immortal in a different way. No more than this will I say, for this is all they understand themselves. When Finns are killed they go to a special place of 'waiting.' There they stay for an unknown length of time. When they have served their time they will return to this world in the same form as they once were. As such, they too will one day be both beloved as angels and despised as demons for having no soul." Lutrin shuddered. "But those with a third eye can see me if they wish. I can be seen in the shapes made by the plants and trees, and in shafts of light."

Pan's words that afternoon had disturbed Lutrin deeply. He went to see Lucknow. They shared a meal together and Lucknow served him some tea. He had no desire for ale or his pipe that night. Just before he went home, he embraced Lucknow and kissed her goodnight.

'That kiss. That embrace. My love.' These were the last three things Lutrin remembered that night before bedtime. 'Oh, what a wonderful night's sleep,' he thought as went deeper and deeper into sleep.

On waking, Lutrin gently rocked from side to side. 'That was a good night's sleep ... or am I still dreaming?' His hand felt wet.

"Get up you lazy faggott," were the first words Lutrin heard that morning. He jumped up to find he had been laying at the bottom of a long-boat.

"Steady now. Three days and nights you've been asleep," said an ugly, pox-marked, nasty piece of work. Lutrin felt cold and disorientated. As his eyes became accustomed to the light he noticed a shoreline to his west, with a treacherously high cliff.

He had seen this image with his tura when he was a child. Before one reached the cliff wall, a series of islets could be seen bordering the coastline. The long-boat drifted towards one of the islets. Within minutes, people were burning little fires, began shouting, and then started firing arrows at the boat. "Damn Doggi", said the ugly man, "they're a stubborn lot." Lutrin laughed. "Don't be laughing too loud. If you wake one of these warriors, special or not, you'll be in for a beating."

Almost awake, Lutrin took in all his surroundings. He was on a boat. A long-boat full of villains, heading north. He looked at his hands. He looked at his arms. Confused, he sat down. 'I am a little child again,' he thought. 'Why did I 'think' this. Unless I did not. Was it Amergin's doing?'

"Stop day dreaming," said the man, "and throw the line-out. These guys eat raw fresh fish for breakfast." Lutrin complied, and hauled in many fish. Then, from the corner of his eye, he saw a Dogger fishing boat. Immediately, Lutrin dived into the sea.

It was cold, but that was the last thing on his mind. He swam as fast as he could and grabbed the side of the Doggers' boat.

"Help me," cried Lutrin, as a Dogger hit hard on his fingers with a water-bailer.

"We don't get involved. Sorry lad."

Lutrin held on to the side. "I am of noble birth. It will be worth your while," he pleaded.

"Sorry again lad," said the man as he kicked Lutrin's fingers, "it's the law."

"Whose law?"

"Fecir's law."

As his fingers gave way, Lutrin recognised the figure at the back of the boat and, using his tura, spoke directly to him, 'Taesus, it is me, your old friend Lutrin.'

Not looking up, Taesus kept repeating in his head, 'I must still be asleep. I am only thinking that he spoke to me. It is only my imagination or I am still dreaming.'

The foot kicked Lutrin once again, leaving only his left hand to hold on. The boat meanwhile, had drifted towards the fast flowing sea-river that ran southwards between the islets and the cliff wall. "Pull her back Fecir. Go along that dangerous route and heaven knows where we will end up," said another man seated by Taesus. This gave Lutrin a little longer to hold on, now that Fecir wasn't kicking him.

"Shut your mouth," said Fecir to the man. "I know my own waters."

"Taesus," Lutrin shouted, "do not let them get me. It would be the death of you all."

Taesus moved towards him. "Sorry stranger, but to save you could provoke war with the Orci. We look to our own, which is why we survive and always will."

"War will be upon you soon enough. Without me though, your people will surely die."

"So, stranger, or would you have me say 'old friend,' do you promise to save my people?"

"I do so promise."

Taesus felt moved by Lutrin's words. "This is the best I can do," he said, grabbing the rudder and swinging Lutrin's side of the boat close to the sea-river's current. At that moment he kicked Lutrin's fingers, loosening his final grip. Lutrin was caught in the swirl, just as Fecir managed to pull the boat back to safety. Lutrin was too far away to hear Taesus shout, but he heard his words, 'I could do no more. I may have saved your life, if you manage to stay in the centre of the flow. Nobles get given 'The Eagle' in Orcades, and I don't mean the bird.' Taesus lay back in the boat and fell into a deep sleep.

Lutrin was caught in a high-speed rapid. His abilities were of no use here. He needed luck, to keep from being shredded against the cliff face that sped past him. Even if his luck held out, his strength might not. It was hard to keep his head above water and he was tiring.

A faint outline of Pan could just be seen, if anyone was looking. "Come on my beauties," he said, "come on." Two dolphins swam either side of Lutrin and kept nudging him back into the centre of the flow.

A few hours later, Lutrin started to fall asleep. He was trying hard to keep his eyes open.

Lutrin thought he could hear ancient Uralic. 'Ilura latha minen,' it said.

"Ilura latha minen," said a young Finn's voice.

Lutrin tried to see where the sound emanated from.

"Grab hold of the rope," she shouted.

Lutrin instinctively put his hands in the air in the hope of grabbing a rope. Instead, he dropped beneath the waves. An undercurrent caught him and dragged him down. He kept his eyes open. 'Too long without air. Goodbye my love,' he thought as his world became peaceful and calm. He felt as if he was a turtle swimming blissfully as the white shoreline called to him. 'This is not so bad,' he thought, as an upward current brought him to the surface at the exact moment that a hand grabbed his hair and pulled his head up.

The Finns had built a single-file bridge, from their most easterly point, to the Dogger peoples' main island at Doggerbank. Lutrin had been saved by the acrobatic antics of a small she-Elf, by the name of Lucknow.

The white gulls had warned her of Lutrin's plight. Who had imparted this knowledge to them though, the gulls didn't say. Lucknow had tied a rope from the bridge that spanned the chasm. She climbed down the rope and waited for Lutrin to pass by.

After Lucknow had caught him, she tied the bottom of the rope around him and climbed, exhausted, back up to the bridge. Lutrin was left dangling at the end of the rope.

As she got to the top and sat down to catch her breath, a man came running along the bridge.

"Quick Robin, pull him up." Robin was a tall young man with protruding teeth and large ears.

"If it's one of your knots Lu then he ain't going anywhere," he said, gaily swinging his arm from side to side.

"You do not understand. Look."

(Meanwhile, Pan was looking on. 'You are on your own at this point. I must keep the balance.')

As Robin looked down, he could see why Lucknow was anxious. A shark was swimming along to take up the bait. Robin pulled on the rope just in time. Meanwhile, Lutrin saw the shark lunge at him. As it did so, it closed its eyes. In doing so, it didn't see its prey being snatched from the jaws of death.

Lutrin was buzzing with adrenalin. All his tiredness had gone as he almost ran up the rope to the bridge. Without any conscious thought, he jumped over Robin and gave Lucknow a hug.

"Have we met?" said a startled Lucknow.

"Yes. I mean no, but we will do. Well, we just have. Thank you L..," he stopped himself from uttering her name. Turning to Robin, he said "and thank you too." Silent for a few seconds, he closed his eyes and said, "I will apologise to the shark for losing his dinner today."

"It must be a Pictish thing," whispered Robin to Lucknow.

"No, he is teasing you," she responded, as Lutrin started laughing.

"Thank you both again. My name is Lutrin. Friends call me Lu. Oh, your words were music to my ears. Is it Uralic?"

"It is. You are are a learned fellow to recognise the sound of ancient Finni. You must be an 'Aelfinwine'?" said Lucknow.

"Yes, I am 'Finn friend'." Lutrin looked at Robin. "And your name my good man?"

"Close enough. The name's Goodfellow, Robin Goodfellow; Father of Herne. And this is Lucknow, the daughter of Aniel."

"Lucknow. Robin. What is this?" shouted a stern looking Aniel.

"Father, we saved Lutrin from from the sea."

On recognising the name, Aniel said, "Quick. Get him across the bridge before any Orci see him."

They raced along the bridge and into Belevedon.

"So, you are Lutrin, son of Brude I believe?"

"You know my father?"

"Yes. I know of your ancestry. Tell me Lutrin, can you remember what happened to you. What brought you here?"

"It is a bit hazy, but I think Amergin may have handed me over to Norbold of the Orci."

"I feared as much."

"Why?"

"Because he said that he was considering such a move against you. I told him it would be unwise."

"The thing is," said Lutrin, "I should be getting home and back to my own t...."

"Town. Yes," interrupted Robin, "and with Aniel's permission I would like to travel back with you to the er ... Pict town."

"I agree," said Aniel, "and I shall send a message by gull to Volas."

"Thank you," said Lutrin.

"Goodbye Lucknow. I have a feeling that we shall meet again someday."

"I would welcome your friendship," she replied.

*

Robin and Lutrin set off on the long journey home, heading west by north-west. Lutrin had been pondering his current situation and was walking with his head down. Robin was walking behind him. As they trudged along, Lutrin began to notice that the sound from Robin's footsteps was changing. Instead of flopping feet he could hear .... clip ... clop. Lutrin smiled to himself and stopped, to wait for 'Robin' to catch up.

"Is that you Pan?" asked Lutrin.

"Ha. It took you long enough. Robin Goodfellow indeed. Herne's father!"

"What happened to me Pan? What threw me back in time?"

"You were sleep-walking. Malceni saw you going onto a light bridge, but he was too late to either intervene or see where you went. You needed me. Yes me, the great god Pan. Did I tell you that is what they will call me one day?

Disgusting isn't it?" He looked at Lutrin, hoping that he would agree with him. Lutrin just nodded; he was more interested in knowing what had happened to himself. "It took me three days of scouring time for you. Nuisance. Most people like to drift off to the land of Nod, which is an easy place to find. But you. You. Ah."

"I was thinking," replied Lutrin.

"There you go again, 'thinking'," interrupted Pan, "instead of doing. Just get on with it. You think Amergin is bad. So, the next opportunity you have, act."

"Shall we go home now?"

Someone was staring at them from behind a bush. As Lutrin looked back, he thought that the man recognised him. "Pan, do you see .... ."

"Yes, I do. Time to go."

Lutrin knew that Pan had recognised the person; but before Pan could put a wall over his thoughts, Lutrin heard the name, 'Tibias'. Lutrin had only told Malceni, but he had been looking for Tibias for a long time. It was too late. Pan had pulled the mists around them and, later, although Lutrin didn't know it, he forgot that he'd seen Tibias. But Pan knew that Lutrin's tura was strong, and that eventually he would remember seeing Tibias. He also knew that Lutrin would be very cross with him. 'I'll cross that bridge when I come to it,' he thought.

"Well, now it is time to get you home," said Pan.

Lutrin looked Pan in the eyes. "Why are so good to me?"

As Pan ushered Lutrin onto a light bridge home, he said, "'Nara,' in the old tongue meant womb-sharer. Your aunt Senga is a 'nara' with Volas. 'Pa-nara', meant father-sharer.

When you call someone a 'panara' it means that they are your sister through the father's line only." As he finished speaking Pan had his tongue in his cheek. "Well off you go," he said.

"No," said an astonished Lutrin, "you are joking. Aren't you?" Not knowing whether he wanted to believe it or not. If so, it didn't matter, in as much as Brude was still his physical father. It just meant that Pan had a 'spiritual' involvement somehow.

"See you later," shouted Pan, as the bridge took Lutrin back to Sunna and back to his own time.

*

On his arrival home, he realised that no one knew he had been away. Later that night Lutrin asked Volas about the nature of Pan.

"What's he been saying to you? No, wait, I know. He suggested to you that he is your father?"

"He did intimate that yes."

"He is a cheeky one, remember that. There is a spiritual link between us because when I was young I fell in love with him, just for a short time. That all changed when I met Brude. Before that however, my tura was all over the place and sometimes got caught up with Pan's work. Pan is a nature spirit after all. The link was strong enough to alter you slightly, but nothing more. He would like to think that he is the father of everything that walks on two legs," she said laughing, "and on one level he does have a very paternal side to him. He loves everything."

Lutrin said nothing.

Volas looked puzzled. "Oh, Panara", said Volas, "oh, I

am sorry. I see now, you wanted so much for her to be your sister. Now look Lutrin, it is what goes in your heart that matters. For a while, Pan's mischief gave you a sister, so just hold that feeling and it will always be true."

Lutrin heard a snuffling sound behind him. Lucknow was crying. "What is it my love?" he said.

"Nothing. At least not any more."

"Oh Lucknow," said Volas, "you had been thinking that .... ?"

"Yes," she interrupted, "because of the pendant that he wears. It looks so real and she is so beautiful. I thought Lutrin loved Panara more than me."

"I do love Panara," said Lutrin spluttering, "but, well ... not like that .. you know. She is half a horse. Oh for Manni's sake Lucknow, that would not be right now would it. Besides, since I grew up, we have not seen each other for a long time. She obviously has her own life to get on with. Either that or she just got bored with me."

Lucknow stopped crying and started laughing.

"Would you like me to stop wearing it?" he asked.

"No, really, I think it brings you luck," replied Lucknow.

"Volas," called Brude, "where is that blessed heather ale you promised?"

"Just coming. Hang on a minute. I never said that I was getting it," scowled Volas. "You and Lutrin go and get those dishes washed before you settle down."

'These pesky Finnic plates,' thought Brude. 'Why can't we go back to using throw-away leaves?'

'We heard that,' chorused Volas and Lucknow.

Chapter 7: **DOGGER-'TIES'**

It was summertime, and in a couple of months the Gap would be passing through the new village. It was also the time that Taesus visited them.

"Greetings old friend," said Lutrin. "Come on in."

A tired looking Taesus entered into Lutrin's tree house, which was next to Lucknow's.

"This is a fine place," he said, sitting down, "I see you have acquired a few human comforts?"

"Yes," laughed Lutrin, "it was Lucknow's Elfin that pointed out I may enjoy some luxury."

Taesus stared around the tree. Lutrin's idea of luxury was simple indeed, but he did have a mattress and a pillow. He also had a proper door on his tree, because he found that the bed would get damp with just the usual reed windbreaker in the entrance. This meant additional lighting was needed. He stopped any further renovations, because he noticed that whenever Lucknow acquired anything new for her tree, she would only need something else after that. It was as if there was a spirit that compelled people to amass one thing after another.

'Greed,' Brude called it. 'Having a life,' is how Malceni viewed it. 'Strike a balance' is how Pan responded.

Lucknow appeared in the doorway, "Lu, would you like some tea? How about you Taesus?"

"I would be honoured. Never have I tried it."

Lutrin sat back and pulled out a pipe, which he filled with bits of dried leaves. Taesus jumped up, "Wael-rec. That will kill me if you puff that out in here. Humans are not immune to the 'Tajem Leaf'."

Lutrin smiled, "This is an off-shoot, a different type of leaf. Pan amended the structure of the 'Tajem Leaf' and grew a harmless leaf, that which we call the 'Leaf of Pan'."

"Aha," said Taesus, "you Picts can not be harmed from this new pipe-leaf but humans can."

"How so?"

"Pan provided me with a few barrels for my father to trade with the Orci. They can't get enough of it. However, we know that people who puff away with it may get black lung rot."

"How do you know what it did to their lungs?"

"I have seen the blood eagle ritual, or what their victims looked like afterwards. Trust me, they had lung rot. I hope you never see such a sight."

"That is awful."

"Yes. A dreadful sight."

"No," said Lutrin, tongue in cheek, "I meant not having the ability to transmute the leaf. I would miss my pipe. However, I will not puff inside."

"The Orci Shamans can transmute the leaf."

Lutrin looked like he was going to confess something. "The leaf dampens the power of my tura."

"And that's supposed to be a good thing?" quizzed Taesus.

"In my case, yes. The veils are thin with me. I see so much. The pipe-leaf keeps me grounded, in this reality."

"Tea is outside," called Lucknow.

As they left the tree house, Taesus acknowledged what a lovely area they lived in. Lucknow had arranged some stools around a little table with wooden mugs on them, full of hot tea. She also brought a plate full of hot buttered potatoes. Taesus took his sandals off and joined them with bare feet on the soft cool grass. The trees overlooked a lake with a mountain range in the distance.

"Why would you want to leave here?" asked Taesus. He looked at peace with himself.

"I told you in Athelney. Choice. But there is more. Lucknow and my race do not 'belong' anywhere already established. We need our own new land, to start building something good."

"I understand you will be staying a few nights," said Lucknow. "Has Lutrin shown you your bedding?"

"No, I have not. Come friend, and see my efforts at home-building."

Lutrin led Taesus down the embankment. "Look at this," he said, pointing to a door in the side of a hill. Lutrin had built a house into the hillside. It had a round front door and round windows. Part of the roof extended from the hill, but Lutrin had put turf on it. The chimney came out through the top of the grassy mound. Taesus was surprised. "Around Athelney," continued Lutrin, "the trees are not yet mature enough to be lived in."

Taesus entered the hole in the ground. Smooth stone slabs had been laid throughout. 'Tibboha's house,' thought Lutrin to himself. "The good thing is, is that if you want another room all you need is a spade."

"Once I settle in here I shall not want to leave," joked Taesus. They sat down outside and Lutrin lit his pipe. He blew some leaf-circles to amuse the faeries, who would fly in and out of the rings.

Taesus could never imagine leaving this spot.

Lutrin knew what he was thinking. "I'll tell you what my friend. When we have moved and all the changes we know are coming have happened, I shall give this house to you." Taesus bowed his head in thanks.

After supper they opened a keg of beer that Taesus had brought with him. "I have a favour to ask," said Taesus.

"I have given you a house already, what more do you want?" queried a slightly tipsy Lutrin.

"For yourself and Malceni to visit Dogger. I tried warning them about the sea. Perhaps the sight of you, especially if, you know, perform a little magic, might persuade them."

"Perform a little magic," repeated Lutrin. "Am I a performing seal?" he laughed. "Yes, of course, if Lucknow does not mind."

"We are not yet bonded," she said, "and even then you will still be your own master."

Taesus smiled, "A rare maiden indeed. You are lucky Lutrin."

"Yes I am," he said. "I am blessed."

"As I am my own mistress," she added.

They talked long into the night, long after the ale had gone. Lucknow related the story of her first 'Urinox' with the Picts. "It was all a bit scary at first," she said, "with all these dead people walking into the house. And later I saw Lutrin with his head in a bowl of water. Children were gathered around him and were laughing as his head went up and down."

"I was dookin' for apples," grinned Lutrin, "and I used my horns to flick some apples to those who were having trouble in getting one."

"We have a similar night," said Taesus, "but we can't actually see the dead ancestor."

"Perhaps that is because you celebrate the occasion rather than experience it," said Lutrin.

"How so?"

"Humans follow the sun calendar and choose the same night every year. Picts and Gridolers follow the Moon calendar. But in the Bryhery Gap our wise-healers understand the complex relationship between the two and follow a Moon-Sun cycle."

*

The following week, it was time for them to make the long journey to Dogger, or at least that is what Taesus and Lucknow thought. Only Malceni suspected otherwise, but said nothing.

"Why have you packed all those things?" asked Lutrin cheekily.

"You leave today," said a surprised Lucknow.

"The knapsack, with a change of tunic and the packed lunch is enough."

Taesus looked up, "Are you not coming?"

"Yes, but I have decided to 'perform a little magic' as you call it."

"Excellent," said Malceni, "You've been getting better at this. What do you need now?"

"Light. Always light, and enough water to get a shimmer. Watch this."

From outside his front door, Lutrin opened a bridge into the air. "See you in a few days Lucknow my love. Come on Taesus. Dogger is just over the bridge."

Taesus stepped gingerly onto the bridge of light and followed Lutrin and Malceni. "That's fantastic," said Taesus.

"Which way is it Taesus?" asked Malceni.

"It's across that narrow bridge over there," said Lutrin.

"You've been here before?"

"Let's say, I know this place. We are by the outskirts of the Finnic town of Alauna on the Carnonacae peninsula, near the Boderiae estuary of the Itis river," replied Lutrin.

"I'll take that as a 'yes' then."

They passed through the gateway and crossed the bridge from Belevedon, passing through a second gate to enter the Doggerbank town of Bannatia. Lutrin wondered if the gates were to keep people in, or out. Taesus noticed his interest.

"It is only an Orci precaution," he said, stepping onto what should have been dry land. "Ah, I see it must have rained recently."

Doggerbank shimmered in the sunlight. It was covered with a thin layer of water. The ground was more gravelly than muddy, nevertheless the mess it made was almost as bad. This was obviously a common occurrence. Using wooden planks, a track on raised stilts had been laid out to connect various building and houses. As they walked further inland, it was clear that certain areas were more affluent than others because the track had rotted in places. Behind every building was a channel that served two purposes. Firstly, it acted as the Doggers sewage system and, secondly, it eased the problem of flooding.

They noticed some people were pushing each other around outside one large building. They didn't bother any passers-by and the passers-by didn't bother them either.

"What is that place?" asked Malceni.

"It's a pub," said Taesus. "A little too early to go in there though. Besides, it is a little rough in that one."

A man staggered out of the doorway and stumbled into Lutrin. "Hey," said Lutrin, "watch it Fecir."

Fecir had been drinking a lot. He looked around and couldn't see who was speaking. Lutrin tapped him on the hip. He looked down and tried to focus on Lutrin. "Aah," he screamed, "a ghost," and ran off.

"How do you know Fecir?" asked Taesus.

Lutrin frowned. "A long story, one that you should have remembered," he said, walking away. Malceni and Taesus looked at each other and followed after Lutrin.

The land started to rise up and meet the end of the tracks, which now developed into streets. A signpost read, 'Welcome to Pinnata Castra: Historical home of the Decantae River Tribe'. This was a much more exclusive area, for the sewage channels were covered, and the land had been paved with smooth stones. The people wore much cleaner clothes, and the 'pubs' looked more friendly. The houses were also larger and brighter.

Taesus stopped outside a small, but nevertheless imposing building. "This is the town hall," he said, "where our leader works. He is not expecting us for some time but he will probably see us."

They entered the chief's office and were motioned to be seated. The man looked up and smiled, "Well, what can I ..... ." Recognition and delight grew in his eyes. "Lutrin, is that you?"

"Robin", replied Lutrin jumping to his feet, "Robin Goodfellow. It's great to see you again." Robin was dressed in a bright red full-length tunic, but he also wore leather trousers underneath it and a cardigan around his shoulders.

"Why, you have grown into a handsome young man, I mean Pict, haven't you?"

"What is going on here?" asked Malceni. Taesus' jaw dropped.

"Why, I helped save this little feller from drowning many years ago. Isn't that so Lu. Apparently," continued Robin, "some villains left him to drown when he was just a lad."

Taesus turned somewhat pale and sat down. 'I thought that was a dream,' thought Taesus.

'Not so,' thought Lutrin, 'but don't concern yourself with that now.'

"Are you Okay Taesus?" asked Robin, "I've missed you."

"Sorry, yes, long journey, and .. I missed you too." Taesus stood and gave Robin a hug.

"Well, when you said a Pict was coming to see me I thought you meant one of those bald headed chaps with dirty feet."

Malceni gave him a foul look.

"Well I was surprised that you disappeared. Here I was rescuing you and then I fell asleep. Fell asleep. Why, Aniel was right mad with me. But he had messages sent to him to say that you were okay."

"You know why we are here?"

"I will get straight to the point. There is nothing I can do. They won't budge, and because the sea hasn't risen all year they think that they are okay. I have been making preparations. At least for the Doggerbank folk. Those further north are more isolated. Did you know that our string of islands stretches all the way to the Tyne. Anyway, people of like mind have been helping me move supplies over the bridge. Aniel is taking care of it."

"He is a good person," said Lutrin.

"One of the best I know."

"Thoth will strike soon. You have had your warning."

Robin nodded and shrugged his shoulders.

Later that night, much to Malceni's delight, they went to a pub called 'The Green Man.' Word had been sent to Aniel, but he was too far away to join them. Tarquin turned up though, with his lyre. Robin joined them and sat next to Taesus. Malceni gave Lutrin an odd look that neither with words nor turas required explanation. Lutrin pulled Malceni to one side. "I don't know, I don't want to know, and I don't care," he said.

"I was only thinking", replied Malceni.

"Well don't think too loud, or he will hear you." They both pulled out their pipes.

"That's not allowed," said the barman, "not in here. There's a courtyard out back for that sort of thing."

"Good idea," said Robin, "it is a lovely night outside. The courtyard overlooks the sea."

"What a beautiful sunset," said Taesus.

"The last Dogger will see," said Tarquin.

"What do you mean?" quizzed Robin.

"We Finns feel the land with our spirit. It is trembling,"

"I don't feel anything," mused Taesus.

Tarquin continued, "Within a day, the earthquake is coming. The ice-cap, just to the side and below of the Orcades, is brittle. It will shatter and, instead of a steady drip, you will suffer a deluge."

"If this is Doggers last night," said Robin to Taesus, "let's make it a night to remember."

"Or forget. As is so often the case with humans," teased Tarquin.

Despite the pipe-puffing, other people came and sat in the courtyard. They did so in part because they had never seen Picts before, and also because the sight of one such as Tarquin playing a lyre in the pub was something never heard of either. "They are stubborn," said Tarquin, "inside, they know their doom is coming. They just won't admit that they are beaten."

"Would you Tarquin? Could you? Dogged they may be, yet this is the only home they've known,"said Robin.

"But they shun our help," he protested.

"If they accepted it, they would feel forever in your debt."

Malceni spoke up, "If they had a new land, where no one else has lived, would they go?"

"There's no safe place across the straits," said Taesus, "before Dogger was cut off by the straits, it was joined to the big land over the channel."

"And what of this land?" enquired Lutrin.

"From here, further than the eye could see, the land was full of animals. My ancestors lived like wild animals. Forced to hunt in packs. The land was full of strange and exotic beasts. Cats as big as cattle, with long teeth, and woolly elephants with long tusks."

"But they've disappeared now," said Lutrin.

"From here, yes, but not from across the channel. They have been sighted from our fishing boats. Some still try to swim across the whale-road. No, we have no place to go."

"I know of a place," said Malceni, "well, three places actually but only one worth ... ."

"If we went north of Tyne the Orci would destroy us or, if not the Orci, the large white bears that stray from the ice-caps," said Robin irritably.

"That's one down, two to go," said an approaching voice. It was Fecir. He nodded to Taesus, who nodded back.

"Nice to see you sober Master Fecir," said Robin, resuming his composure.

"Aye. May I join you?" No one said anything. Fecir felt their hostility, but he was used to it. "Just for a short while," he continued. Robin nodded.

"And south-west of Sunna is out of the question," said Lutrin.

"One to go," said Malceni, "and the one place more suitable to the Doggers. A place where Picts would like to have allies."

"I believe your stories," butted in Fecir, "I have made provisions near Tyne. If you know of a place to go then please speak."

"It would have to be agreed by my father," said Lutrin hesitantly, "but if you give an oath of allegiance to all free folk then I am sure he will agree."

"Aniel," said Tarquin, "will gladly help all Doggers."

"All?" said Fecir.

"As I have said."

"Where is this land?" Robin asked Malceni.

"It is north-west of Sunna. The northern most part of Ru is called Hronesness. It is a rugged and beautiful place where precious stones adorn the beaches. No one lives there."

"There seems to be no time to ask permission of Brude," said Tarquin. "Unless .... ." He turned to Lutrin.

"I will gladly do it," smiled Lutrin, "but get me another pint, I shall be thirsty when I get back." Lutrin left the table and, when no one was looking, he nipped in behind the bar and made a bridge to yesterday's Bryhery Gap. Brude agreed with his plan and Lutrin opened a bridge back to the pub. "It is done. Brude agrees," said Lutrin, returning to his seat.

Taesus and Malceni burst out laughing. Tarquin was smiling. They realised what he had done.

Fecir cracked his knuckles and leaned forward in his chair. "Are you trying to be funny?" he said. "Even if you sent word by bird, no message would be back yet."

"A poor joke Lutrin, given the situation we are in," said Robin, disappointedly.

Aniel suddenly walked into the courtyard, with a black-back gull on his shoulder. "I received your father's message this afternoon Lutrin, he said you would be here at this time." Aniel knew Fecir was a rough man but, in the right circumstances, Fecir had good within him. He decided to keep Fecir sweet. "It is an honour Master Fecir, to finally meet the leader of the northern Doggers."

"Why, thank you."

"Do you speak any of the birds' tongues. That of the gull, for example?"

"I'm fluent in the gulls', sparrows' and thrushes' tongues."

"Excellent. Just as one would expect of a distinguished leader. Go and prepare your people for the exodus tomorrow. I presume you can island hop in time?"

"Not possible," said Fecir.

Lutrin gave Taesus a nod.

"Will you trust me?" asked Taesus.

"A man always hopes he can trust his son." The others pretended not to be shocked, but it did explain how Fecir knew where to look for him that night.

"Put on this blind-fold and hold Lutrin's hand."

Fecir hesitated but then shrugged his shoulders. Fecir felt that Lutrin had only walked him to the other side of the courtyard.

Lutrin let go of his hand. "You can take off the blind-fold now."

As he did so, he noticed Lutrin was gone, and that he was on his own island of Tamia in the north. 'Bless me,' he thought, 'my Taesus does have strange friends,' "Good for him," he said smiling. 'If all goes well,' he thought, 'I'll pledge not to drink another drop of ale'.

Back in 'The Green Man,' the humans drank, whilst the Picts puffed away on their pipes. People danced and sang. Later, they asked Tarquin to play a song.

'The Doggertie Island Anthem'

Long did they live on the sand;
Long did they grind.

Until no longer they remembered; Whence from they once come.

Unchanging were they;
Unto even their doom,

But change forced upon them; the free land of Ru.

The earth expanded,
And the ice exploded,

And Dogger was Sunken, beneath the great ocean.

Forever they'll now live,
In the land of the free.

Those red-headed people, the stubborn Doggertie.

Oh, those noble of people, The dogged Doggerties.

Throughout the head-clearing song, the people gradually stood in silence. If they had known the words, they would surely have sang as well. The Pub descended into a respectful silence. Sobbing could be heard, but no tears are shed by the Doggerti. They filed out into the night and home to their beds. "Well, that's one way of emptying the place," said Malceni.

"I liked it," said Robin. "You know, when you referred to us as Doggerties."

"It was an entwining of words," said Tarquin. "All of your people have 'ties' to Dogger".

"We spell it 'tae'. Meaning 'tight', close-knit, or 'tie'".

"Whereas a 'tie' in Uralic is a path, or a way that one follows," said Tarquin.

"In Pictish," said Lutrin, "it means all of them. As you can see from the 'Tae' in Taezali. It is the way of all Zali's to the follow the path of the Bryhery Gap; in doing so our tribe is also close-knit."

"It would appear that all words originated in Pict-turas," laughed Robin. "Seriously though, when we move to our new home, we shall all be known as Doggertaes, in memory of our common homeland."

*

'As Tarquin predicted, an enormous earthquake erupted in the north. The Doggerland would soon be lost and its people forgotten for over eight thousand years. But where did these people go. This is the story of a dogged people who came from Doggerbank beneath the north sea.'

"Great," said Malceni, who was reading a story in Lutrin's mirror, "just great, but what happens to me?"

Lutrin frowned, "You must try harder. Concentrate."

"Okay, yer. Oh, what am I doing? I don't care anymore."

"Excellent," said Lutrin, "you keep hold of the mirror for a while. You are ready at last. But you do remember that it is you creating the images. There is nothing special about the mirror."

"I know. I know. I'm using it as a medium through which my own power bears fruit."

"Well done."

*

The ground began to shake. It was a few minutes to sunset. The shaking became more violent. Despite the obvious danger, most people went to the cliff's edge and looked out over Dogger for the last time. With no people there it gave off an eerie feeling because they could see the empty buildings. Some of them had left candles burning, so that they could see their own houses from the cliffs. It became deathly silent. No baby cried. No dog barked. No bird sang. The shaking stopped. They could see no change. Some of them wanted to go back home.

"Steady now," shouted the sober Fecir, "steady."

And then came the sound from far off. A screeching, scraping, horrible sound. Followed by the wave. The people could not turn their eyes away. The wave was almost as tall as the cliffs. They could see seals and whales being tossed about. And then came the crash of the water over Doggerland. The sun set. Dogger was no more.

A new sea was born. A cold and cruel sea. The sea of Thoth. And then the tears did come. The people did cry and the people did wail. Homeless and lost. 'But not forgotten, thought Lutrin, 'nothing is ever forgotten.' Slowly, but surely, the Doggertaes began their long trek to Hronesness. Lutrin could not help them. Light bridges took too much energy from him and there was no way he could keep a bridge open long enough for them all to cross.

*

"Why did you finally let me look after the mirror?" asked Malceni.

"Oh Malceni, my friend, you are a breath of fresh air when all around is gas. People applaud me as a light, but you are the breath. You can live for a while without the light, but not the breath. With your jokes and silly remarks you achieved here today what the wise could not. You have saved an entire race of beings from extinction. I helped you. It wasn't you helping me. And now I say this, keep the mirror and its secrets. They are yours, for good or ill."

"Thank you," said Malceni, "but now I feel funny. I don't know what to say."

"One last thing Mal. When the song or story of our lives is written, I will do my best to make sure that you are treated as an equal and I am not given all the glory."

'Explain, please,' thought Malceni who tended to fall back

on his tura when things became a little complicated.

Lutrin laughed. 'Never mind, it is fine.'

*

It was agreed that all Doggertaes would meet in the Belevedon Midlands. Fecir took three weeks to arrive. On arrival he told Taesus that he had taken the pledge. Malceni also heard him apologising to Taesus for some past misgiving; but of what they were, he did not say.

By this time, Lutrin wanted to go home.

"You could always jump home. What is your problem?" asked Malceni.

"It is what Taesus once said about the 'journey' being important."

"Yes. And he's right for part of the time, but it's a gift you have Lu. As long as you don't abuse it you will still have journeys. I know, if we haven't finished here in two weeks, you will go back."

"Don't you want to see the Gap arrive?"

"Lu. I was kept in the Gap far longer than you. Look at us, these humans might think I am your younger brother. They don't know we are the same age."

"I have never looked at it like that."

*

The Doggertaes had made good progress and were only about one week from the Eyribol Ridge. Along the way, the Finns had fed them and now, to their surprise, the Gridolers did also. Robin was in good spirits and suggested Lutrin and Malceni went home. In the end, Taesus went with them as well.

"A few days indeed." Lucknow pretended to look cross. "Come here," she said, and kissed him.

"Before we go and rest," said Malceni, "I have a request to make of you." Lucknow made ready to leave. "No," he continued, "it involves you as well Lucknow. Please stay." They all sat down on the grass outside the tree house and waited for Malceni to begin. He enjoyed this feeling of comradeship. "I want us all to go on a journey together."

"No problem, I can open a bridge for us."

"You can't Lu," replied Malceni, "this is the one place that you have been unable to find."

"You mean, look for .... him?"

"Yes. And I think Taesus has an interest also."

"Oh yes, he might, after the song he sang for us."

"Don't keep Lucknow and myself in the dark any longer you two. Out with it."

"What does 'Tibias' mean to you?" asked Malceni.

"Who is Tibias?" asked Lucknow.

"Tibias is old magic," said Taesus, "he counseled my mother when she could not give birth."

"And what has this to do with me?" asked Lucknow.

"The Finns kept it from the Elfin," said Lutrin. "For some reason they felt shame and spoke no more of Tibias after you were born."

"You see," said Malceni, "Tibias also helped some Finns and Picts."

Knowledge of the implications of this struck her immediately. "And I suppose Volas was helped as well." They nodded.

"Well," she said, "adventures should not always be the domain of the male. As soon as the Doggertaes are safe in their new land we shall all go and seek out this Tibias character."

"Yes", said a delighted Malceni, "about time I got to choose."

*

There was still a week before the Gap arrived. This meant that the Doggertaes would not see it. They knew nothing about the Gap in any case. The Picts would meet them on Eyribol Ridge and provide them with enough provisions to get them through the oak forest. Then they would have to fend for themselves. It is said that they were the only refugees in the history of mankind, where none died of starvation or lack of care. It was clear that apart from being given food, the Doggertaes could look after their own. It was still summer, thankfully, but it meant that they needed to arrive in plenty of time, before winter, to set up new homes. The Picts had already made trips up north and were able to advise Robin on places of shelter where necessary.

It was the Finns however that shortened their journey. When they arrived in central Eyribol, the Finns were waiting with many ships to sail them around the coast. And so, at last, the Doggertaes arrived at their new home and immediately set to making it their own.

Chapter 8: **TIBIAS**

Winter came and went. The spring was here. It was time to make preparations for their long journey. However, they didn't know where their destination was, as yet. It was time to ask Pan for assistance in their quest to find Old Tibias.

"But why? Why do you want to see Tibias?" Asked Pan.

"I'd have thought it was obvious", replied Taesus, who believed Pan was deliberately being evasive.

"You appear to have trouble hearing me," said Pan taking a step backwards.

'Careful now,' thought Malceni, 'Push him and he will just go the opposite way.'

"That is very wise Malceni," said Pan.

"Sensible", he replied, mimicking Pan. "Must keep a balance."

"You know," said Lucknow smiling innocently, "that we will go, with or without your help. Without it and we may take far more time than we should. You wouldn't want that would you."

Pan's eyes showed signs of a wavering intent.

Lutrin turned his back and started to walk away. "We will start in the Marches," he called to the others. "That is were I saw him."

Pan put his head down and headed slowly toward Lutrin. "You must understand. I did it ... ."

"It's okay. Really," said Lutrin, "you haven't trusted me since that day I went to walk over the first light bridge I made. I did not say so at the time, but I was about to look where I was going."

"Can you remember how to get to that first place you saw?" asked Pan.

"No. Of course not."

"Pity. It would save you a lot of time."

"You don't mean?"

"Yes. I was amazed at what you did and then realised that Tibias probably had something to do with it." Lutrin looked furious. "I was protecting you. You were not ready to see him then."

"Tibias obviously thought he was," sneered Malceni.

"So typical," said Pan. "What a fickle friend you are Malceni. You would trust the judgement of someone you've never met, more than mine."

"It's called faith Pan," said Taesus. "If it wasn't for him we wouldn't be alive."

"Rubbish. You would all be alive, but not in your current form. Do not be so hasty in forming alliances."

"Are you saying Tibias is a bad person?" asked Lucknow.

Pan looked shocked. "Oh no, no, no, no, no. If you meet him you will see that he looks at things in a different way."

"Do you mean, like in the way you that have very little do with wizards?" asked Malceni.

"Very astute of you again. But no. I am concerned for all of you. Tibias doesn't see life in the same way as I do."

"Will you help us?" asked Lucknow.

"I can only give you a general direction. In this case," he said, smiling at Taesus, "the journey is important. You must head for the Lakes near his Kingdom in the Land of Boulders. Do not. I repeat, do not open any light bridges."

"Why not?" asked Lutrin.

"It would be very dangerous. Tibias only allows people to see him when he permits it and if he wants it so."

"And he probably doesn't want to see us now you mean?" asked Malceni.

"He may not because you have been influenced by me and have a love of this world. However, if you keep seeking him, he may allow you into his Kingdom."

"He still sounds unpleasant."

Pan sighed. "No. Just different. Let me tell you, regarding my comment earlier about being fickle. Tibias would actually say, 'how can you love me, whom you have not seen, more than Pan, whom you have. Or something like that anyway."

"Is it okay to go by pony or horse?" interjected Taesus.

Lutrin thought of Panara. 'Where is she now?' he thought, "Pan?" he queried.

Pan had already turned away, partly to hide his tears and also to allow him to cover his thoughts, 'For the greater good I was told not to interfere in this episode. Tibias had better be right about this,' he thought. "Yes," he shouted back, "ponies are fine."

Lutrin said, "Pan. Do you know .... ?"

"Sorry, I haven't a clue. Bye," interrupted Pan.

'That is odd,' thought Lutrin, ' he didn't hear my thoughts. Unless. He must have been wondering about her too.'

*

They loaded up the cart with lots of provisions, including one small tent each for Lucknow and Taesus, and a larger tent for Lutrin and Malceni. Taesus needed his own space because the Picts tura would keep him up all night, especially if Malceni was having that recurring nightmare again. Two ponies pulled the cart with two of the little people on it, with one riding a pony. Taesus rode a horse. And so, with much excitement they set off for Tibias' Kingdom, into the Land of Boulders. "Which way are you going?" asked Pan.

*

Tibias was looking at a criss-cross pattern of light in front of him. He pointed at a gap in one of the lines and smiled when he saw Thoth. "Silly thing," he said.

Thoth looked up. "What, who said that?" he said, with a sudden flash of fear.

Tibias moved his finger a little and saw Lutrin and the others by the cart. "South-west," he whispered.

*

"South-west," they all answered.

"How did we ... ?" asked Taesus.

"That was Tibias," said Pan, rather matter of factly. "A good sign, but it doesn't automatically mean success. Good luck."

"Pan. Oh Pan," came a call from the nearby shore, followed by a lot of giggling.

"Come with us," said Lutrin. More calls and giggles could be heard.

"Must dash," said Pan, pulling his Pipes out. "There are some Water-Lilies that require my attention."

As they left their familiar surroundings, they could hear Pan's pipes drift away to nothing.

They were heading for a part of Ru where no people had gone before. The ground rose steeply before them until they could go no further in that direction. The land plateaued out and, as far as the eye could see, was nothing but a marshy bog. The companions chose to head West because the marsh continued far to the south. Whereas they could see mountains in the West. As such, they desired to go around the mountains in the hope of finding a more hospitable landscape. As it was, they had to risk continuing through the marsh during the night. In darkness, Lucknow was the only one with the ability to see harder ground beneath the sloshing sounds of the water. The others slept in the back of the cart whilst she steered all night, meandering in and out, along an unseen trail. They had to keep moving in case the cart sank.

In the morning, Taesus got a fire going in the back of the cart. All Pict carts carried a large stone bowl for use in cases like this. Lutrin picked up some fish for baking and Malceni swapped places with Lucknow. When she joined Lutrin and Taesus in the cart, she was furious. So furious that they thought her rage might become explosive.

"What is it my love? What ails you on a such a morning as this? Sleep later, after breakfast." She looked even more angry.

"You were the only one Lucknow," said Taesus, "who could guide us through the marshes. None could take your place. All of us here will do our share throughout this adventure. Such is the way with comrades."

'Maybe she shouldn't have come,' thought Malceni, 'Oops. Here it comes.'

She grabbed Malceni's pipe and threw it at him. He infuriated her even more by catching it.

'He's fast,' thought Taesus, 'but I wish he were slower today.' Lucknow grabbed at Taesus' hair ribbon and tugged it into a knot. He could have stopped her of course, but in matters like this Taesus had a better understanding of the opposite sex than either Lutrin or Malceni, especially Malceni. Turning her attention to Lutrin, she grabbed his mug of tea. He winced, half expecting it to land on his head.

"This," she said, "this is what I wanted. All night without being offered anything, or any relief." She jumped off the cart and they all looked the other way. The cart kept moving; which gave Taesus time to think of an excuse.

"I won't lie to her," said Lutrin.

"He did not say 'you' lie. Just keep your mouth and mind closed," said Malceni.

Lucknow ran and caught up with the cart.

"We had no wish to scare you last night," said Taesus, "in case it put you off your steering. I thought we may have been followed and so we kept low and kept listening."

She made no reply, but after her breakfast she said, "I shall sleep now. Anyone who wakes me will end up head first in the bog. Don't worry about anything following us.

With all your snoring last night I am sure it would not have got lost."

As they neared the foot of the mountain, the marsh became solid ground. Fascinated at how she could remain angry for so long, the others remained silent until it started to rain. Low-level black clouds hung heavily in the air and Lutrin pulled a waterproof tarpaulin over Lucknow. Although he had already taken his turn steering, he told Malceni to get under the tarpaulin. The rain continued relentlessly. Taesus offered to take Lutrin's place up-front, but Lutrin declined, saying, "You can only get wet once."

A few minutes later Lucknow finally spoke, "I shall make some tea."

"You could set fire to the tarpaulin," said Taesus, "and without it you couldn't shield the fire from the elements."

"They call me an Elf," she said, "but inside I am Finnic." She went to the stone bowl and, with a few dry leaves and a little straw, created a radiant light from just her breath. She blew again and its heat increased. Shortly after she had made tea for them all, the cart stopped.

"Lu?" called Taesus, as he went to take Lutrin his tea. There was no answer. "Lu?" He popped his head out and noticed it had stopped raining. Being unable to see Lutrin with the reins, Taesus stood up and noticed that Lutrin was lying on the seat. "Lu, what's wrong?" Lutrin lay there unblinking. 'Darkness' descended upon them, so Taesus picked him up and took him inside the cart. "Re-light your fire Lucknow. A foul dread has blighted him. Unnatural it is, for see, the cloud-murk lies heavy before the setting sun."

The 'darkness' seemed to push at them. "Malceni," said Lucknow, "take this, and tie the animals heads in here, under the tarpaulin." She handed him some of the light she had created in her hands. It felt cool to him. "Keep it in front of you at all times."

As Malceni uncoupled the ponies and brought the other two animals with him, he felt fingers touching him. If he allowed any to cling on too long they began to pull at him. The animals were as distressed as he was, but Lucknow's light calmed them enough, for now. When they were all huddled together, Lucknow spoke to the animals, sending them into a standing slumber.

Outside, the shadow-stalker gained a voice. "Come, come," it whispered, "we nearly have you. Come, come."

"What are these terror-mongers, and what do they want?" said Taesus.

"Lutrin has spoken of them before," said Malceni, "they are not evil. It's just a bit of a misunderstanding really. Or, that's what he thinks. He's too scared to think otherwise."

"A misunderstanding," said Taesus, barely believing his ears.

"Some time back, Lutrin was almost killed. He knows that he reversed time, just a fraction of a second, to avoid death. The problem is that it wasn't the first time."

"And he thinks death is looking for him?" asked Taesus.

"Not thinks. Many times he has avoided death. He barely avoided it twice in one week alone soon after he amended time. But the incidents get further apart now. He is a silly thing, going out without his pipe."

"What's his ... ?"

"Why?" said Lucknow, interrupting Taesus.

"Well, these twilight-terrors appear closer when he gets thrown, mentally. It's as if he needs to be completely grounded, or he 'drifts' in-between worlds."

"You said 'closer'," said Lucknow.

"Yes. It is always there. Waiting for him to slip. Leaf-aroma keeps it quite far away. So far at times, he can even forget it's there."

"So, what happened now?" asked Taesus.

"I think that Lutrin, alone, up front, began to shift a little," said Malceni. "Without the usual Pan or Pictish distractions, he probably drifted further than usual towards the other time-line."

"Now you've lost me," said Taesus. Malceni shrugged his shoulders.

"They are trying to take him back to the time-line he avoided," said Lucknow.

"Yes," replied Malceni. "To die. Which means that everything he has achieved, or will do, will cease to be."

"But they appear to want us as well," said Taesus, feeling a little afraid now.

"Naturally," said Lucknow, "they want to take us back to where we would be if Lutrin had died that day."

Malceni indicated that Lucknow should try to get some tea into Lutrin, and then lit his pipe. "Put your head outside if you want to Taesus, this won't take long." Lucknow, Taesus and the animals all looked at him.

"Very funny Malceni. But, I'll be okay for a minute thank you."

Taesus held Lutrin upright whilst Lucknow dripped tea into his mouth. Malceni blew the leaf's aroma under his nose. Lucknow held up her light. The voice stopped calling outside.

"Lutrin," called Malceni, "go towards the darkness. Keep away from the light." Lucknow started to lower her hand. "No," continued Malceni, "keep it there. It is dark here because the 'darkness' has created the opposite in order to entice Lutrin to head for their light. By using all his senses we want him to come back here. I think he will do so because he can see your sacred Finni light, has tasted earthy tea, has smelt the 'Leaf of Pan' and heard my friendly voice. He just needs a kiss."

Taesus nodded and kissed Lutrin quickly.

"Not you," said Malceni, "dear me, I meant Lucknow."

"What was I supposed to think? You'd mentioned everyone else."

Just before Lucknow kissed him, the horse licked Lutrin's face. "Oh Panara," he said, "that tickles."

"Lutrin," said Lucknow.

A bewildered Lutrin jumped up. "What! Where?" he exclaimed.

The 'darkness' had gone and the sun was still high. Before them, to the south, was a gap through the mountain, which looked like the only place they could head for where they could still keep the cart with them. On reaching the top of the ridge to the gap, they could see a pathway, not made by natural means, between two mountains. They could also see a series of lakes, and hoped that they were nearing their goal. It made sense to join the road but, as it was now getting dark, they set up camp for the night a few hundred feet into the gap.

The following morning they had an early start because it was another lovely day. At the bottom of the valley, the road followed the Black Lake's shoreline and out through another mountain gap.

After a further ten miles southwards, they saw the first lake. Eastwards, they noticed a hillside with many boulders and, without further guidance, decided to head in that direction. Mid-way up the hill and it was time to settle down for the night.

*

Pan was talking to Tibias. "Well. It is time for you to decide."

"By the morning they will forget why they came this way," replied Tibias.

"I'll not let you do that to Malceni. He has suffered too much."

"I could make you forget also."

"Very, very dangerous. Either you talk to them or I will," said Pan.

"Perhaps you are right. But I will only interact with them in my more simple physical form."

"Excellent," said Pan.

*

The companions awoke the following morning to find the

field, in which they had camped the night before, had now become a huge garden, full of trees, shrubs and flowers. A house was also standing at the brow of the hill. They smelt food cooking and could hear someone humming a tune. 'I think we've arrived," said Lucknow. "Let us go and see Tibias."

As they approached the house a robed, and hooded, figure stood in front of the doorway. In their heads they heard a voice that was neither male nor female, 'Do not be afraid of what is about to happen,' it said, lowering its hood, 'it is but my first gift to you.' The four stepped forward and instinctively bowed.

As Taesus raised his head he saw nothing behind the hood. 'Put aside your feelings of loneliness Taesus, for you will meet someone soon.'

Each of them saw something different.

A dark skinned unseen face, shrouded in mist, hovered before Malceni. 'My poika', she said, 'forgive me, as you can see I am not exactly a Pict. I left you with Brude because I knew that you would have a better start in life than any life I could give you.' He had almost seen his mother.

'Do not be harsh on your father Lucknow. Giving birth to you sent me to the place of waiting. His grief of that day is renewed each morning that he sees you. The pain is too much for him to bear, which is why he wanted you to live in Sunna.'

Lutrin saw himself sitting on a throne. The people were worshipping and kissing his ring. "Bow before his holiness, Pius II," said a voice to all the women present. He tried to remove the ring of female oppression from his finger, but it was infused into his flesh and bone.

Thoth stood behind him. "Good work my poika," he said.

Lutrin was gasping for breath. 'I can not breathe,' he thought. "Help me," he shouted.

Grappling with the robe, which now fell to the floor, Malceni shouted, "Leave him alone."

Lutrin saw the face of death and then saw no more.

Tibias appeared in the doorway and gently picked Lutrin up. They had to presume it was Tibias, because he kept changing from young to old and from human to Finn. Within these images though, he looked a lot like Amergin, with eyes like ice. Tibias took Lutrin inside the house and laid him on a sofa. "He is fine, really," said Tibias.

"What happened?" asked Lucknow.

"Each of you saw what you secretly feared the most."

"How is that a gift?" said Taesus.

"By acknowledging your fears, you can diminish their power. But you need to recognise them first. The subconscious will do all it can to stop you. For it too has a life to live out. It guides you to behave in a way that it feels will feed itself; be that anger in certain situations or even offering love to another. It has a fear that you will not want it anymore. Although it can appear as darkness, the subconscious is like a child in many ways. Tell it that all will be well. Thank it for what it has done for you in the past, and then say, 'we must move on now, together'. But remember this, when making jests with one another, be careful how you say things, because the subconscious does not understand humour. It believes everything it hears and sees." Lutrin began to wake up.

"Welcome back," continued Tibias. "Your friends here all experienced typical common fears. But you. You see far, further than any physical being ever has." Tibias stood away from the sofa. "I shall tell you all of half of almost everything that you think that you want to know, and later I shall tell you all of almost all of the half that you don't."

They wondered just how much this meant they would hear.

"I was once alone. Oh so alone, in eternity. Alone in the darkness. In despair, I created a world and filled it with good and bad people. Through them, I gave myself purpose and meaning. I lived many lives. You name it, and I did it. Eventually, I had done everything but still found myself alone. A new idea formed; I would create immortal individuality for the 'deserving'. The 'deserving' however, ended up becoming just like me. This led me to create Thoth and his brothers; to be teachers. Before I had a chance to finish their training ... well you know what happened next. But by permitting the existence of immortal individuality, I had created an unsolvable paradox; the future is not just determined now by those actions which happen today. The past is also influenced by the future. The crux of this is, that if you can control human consciousness, by indoctrinating the mind into believing it is powerless, then you may also control the universe. I have become fairly powerless. Future structures are sending individuals back to 'the One', the 'One' being me; and it changes my spirit. As such, there are very few truly individual individuals left and most of them came from a previous world."

Tibias turned to Lutrin. "As one who gained individuality in the world before this one, you are quite safe. Tell them how you achieved this."

Lutrin looked embarrassed, but nodded. "I disbelieved everything I saw and realised that everything was an illusion."

"But surely others have thought so?" commented Malceni.

"Yes, but thinking is one thing, knowing and experiencing is another. Some people will stress it, but they are only doing so because it is what they most need to learn."

"Prior to Lutrin," said Tibias, "anyone who saw through the illusion went mad. To truly know that your world is made of 'no-thing' is hard to take. Only I knew."

Lutrin continued his tale. "But that is what started me off. It was you I saw. All alone. I saw you and felt your pain. The pain was too much for me to bear. Some time later, I knew that 'enlightenment' was just a figment of the imagination. There was no such thing. However, knowing this must have almost been like what people expected of enlightenment. I was happy and content, just 'to be'. Striving was false. Finally, I saw the 'no-thing' you refer to and, instead of going mad, chose to live in my own illusions rather than suffer with the illusions of others."

"Can we eat now?" said Malceni, "we didn't have any breakfast. There is much to ponder on, but my physical needs are a reality!"

Tibias provided them with an endless amount of bread, which was something the Picts were not accustomed to, butter, mushrooms, cakes and tea. Music could be heard but the source was unseen. Near the end of their meal, Tibias handed Lucknow a piece of paper. "This is a little poem I wrote for your people for when you move near the Meare. It doesn't advocate selfishness, but it warns against those who can easily drain your energy," said Tibias.

'The Prayer of the Spirit'

Filling ones life spaces,
With other peoples 'can'ts.'
And taking nothing for oneself,
Is not what Spirit wants.

To freedom have, from servitude,
Is living just to be.
But someone will not like it,
And will stomp on your sovereignty.

Manipulatives will manipulate;
Digging claws in deep.
Draining well earned life force,
So they can live for free.

Broken chains for you are there;
Would you just but say,
"Enough of this, this stops today,
Don't live your life through me."

For all you know, one life you have,
And then it all but goes.
And the memories you've left behind,
Were other peoples goals.

So take the time, to ask yourself,
'What is it that 'I' want?'; not need.
Then seek it out, before your old,
So no resentments will we breed.

"Thank you," she said. 'But a bit gloomy,' she thought.

The view of the mountains and lakes was glorious. Tibias had a horse and cart outside the door, and Taesus had a back-pack with some sandwiches in it. The sun was beating hard upon Malceni's head. "Put this on," said Tibias, passing Malceni a cap. "Take it home with you."

"Thank you," said Malceni, "is it magic?" Tibias just smiled at him and flicked the reins.

They left the cart near the lake and walked to the water's edge. The boatman was already waiting. He was as small as Malceni, with the same skin shade. "In life, he was a Firbolg," said Tibias.

"Is this place real?" asked Lucknow.

Tibias smiled, "And what is real?"

Lutrin knew that she didn't like it when people spoke like this, so he said, "No my dear. It is not real in the way that we are used to. Nevertheless, while we are here it is very real."

The Firbolg rowed them to the other side of the lake where the mountains rose gently from the water. There was little wind, and the mountain peaks were seen reflected on the water's surface. An ancient Fern tree wood stretched along the entire length of the lake. "Follow the white ribbons," said Tibias, as they entered what looked like impenetrably dense vegetation. A stream flowed down the mountain-side and beneath the undergrowth. Even Taesus could stand up when they followed the white ribbons, which were tied onto branches at various places along the path. Up and up they went, until the mountainside flattened out into a boggy area.

A further short climb brought them to a clearing. In the centre stood the oldest tree in the Kingdom.

"She's lovely," said Lucknow.

"I rescued her from the future," said Tibias. "From a world reeking with the stench of unnecessary tree burning."

"Krakto," whispered Lucknow to the tree. At which point a mouse came scurrying out from a crack in the tree. It sniffed at Tibias' feet and then metamorphosed into a beautiful Finni-like (no pointed-ears) woman of light.

"Meet Krakto," said Tibias. "In this form, she is my wife, or 'snuggler' as you might say. To some, she is a goddess; 'Thee Goddess'. In truth we are both manifestations of 'the same One'."

Krakto solidified and became physical. Her eyes were like flaming hot coals. "Greetings," she said. "We do not often have guests anymore. Tibias has been grumpy lately." She tugged a little at his nose. "My little Gridoler," she said.

Malceni leaned over and whispered, "Picnic," in Taesus' ear. Taesus passed him a sandwich.

Krakto looked at Lucknow. "How lovely you have become. More lovely than when you were last here."

Lucknow looked puzzled. "I do not recall that pleasure my Lady."

"Come," replied Krakto, "and I will show you the answers to many questions. They followed her into another clearing and saw it was full of what looked like innocent faeries. "If this reminds you of the Bryhery Gap, then it does not surprise me. It is a similar place and yet different, as are the beings that inhabit it."

They all stared at the little beings and then realised that none of them were interacting or playing with one another. They lived mostly in isolation.

"Such sadness," said Tibias. "They can still move me to tears."

"What is wrong with them?" asked Taesus.

"They have seen terrible things in their lifetimes," said Krakto. "Remember, Bryhery Gap, like here, exists out of time. The faeries could be from the past or future. These little ones though are mainly from the future, and their numbers are growing." Lutrin saw images of bombs falling from the sky, and the murdering of innocent children. "The men, and indeed some women with them, which do such wicked things are more evil than Thoth," she said. "Yes, they come from Thoth's seed, but their ways are their own. Thoth wants power, but these people do it for wealth or 'beliefs'."

Tibias spoke up, "Their past lifetimes have been so awful that they are frightened to reincarnate. In addition, their souls have been infected with linear time. Krakto brings them here for healing. Some will never return. Eventually, we will release them into the woods where they will remain faery." He pointed at one of the beings. It kept changing from one animal to another, and sometimes a hybrid of both. It looked lost and didn't know what to do. "This one is suffering from the imposition of man-made laws on rebirth. If it shows no sign of settling, we will have to wipe out its time-lines."

"And that is not good?" asked Lucknow.

"If we do that it can only return to its home or remain as faery. It may never incarnate again."

"We must stop Thoth," said Taesus.

"Have you not understood anything I have said? Alone, this is not really Thoth's doing. You could say it is mine as well. But that would not tell all. No, this is the result of mass human consciousness that has been manipulated by a group who call themselves the enlightened ones."

"But what have these faeries to do with us?" asked Malceni.

"You were once like them," said Lucknow, "hence that business with the carnelian birth-stone and the tinctures."

"That is right," said Tibias. "In the outside world, hedge-magic can entice these sad ones to return. The magic carries with it two promises. Firstly, that life will be alright and, secondly, that they can become faery again, as soon as possible, if they don't like it."

"In your cases," said Krakto looking at Lutrin and Malceni, "we needed a new species to entice you. You wanted to be different and you wanted to make a difference. We provided you with what you wanted. As for Taesus, you have different needs and they will be met."

"And me," asked Lucknow, "how could I have been here? None of my kind would be seen in a place like this."

Krakto sighed. "We will not even hint at the answer. But I promise you that it will be revealed to you before the end."

Tibias turned to Lutrin and said, "Is that everything?"

"Not quite," he replied, closing off his mind, "I have three more questions for you."

"We shall answer only two," said Krakto.

"You must seek the third answer yourself," continued Tibias.

"Firstly, why do you and Pan not see eye to eye?"

Tibias answered, "We are both right, but can appear wrong to each other. Pan keeps the balance of nature on your planet, and usually within a time boundary."

"Whereas we," said Krakto, "have a more timeless and Universal aspect to consider."

'Which means,' thought Taesus, 'that they might consider some life to be expendable.'

"My second question," said Lutrin, "is this; Pan said he was a conduit. Is this the place of vibrational change he referred to, or is it elsewhere?"

"It is elsewhere," said Tibias. "Some people might hope to reach me here and that is fine, to a point. But change can only come by activating the conduit. Don't you see yet, the place of vibrational change is within you? The signal would go full circle. The very process of the activation with Pan is also the point of change."

"Somebody call me?" It was Pan. "I have missed you all. Would you like a short-cut home. They all nodded and thanked Krakto and Tibias for their hospitality. After stepping through a portal to Sunna, they saw that the ponies and cart were already there. "Lutrin," what was your third question?"

"There wasn't one. I know how these things work," he replied smiling.

"Crafty," said a delighted Pan, "very crafty."

"But there was something I wanted to talk with you about; rather than Tibias." Pan was even more delighted. "What is the 'Ego'?" asked Lutrin.

"The Ego stems from the 'subconscious' that Tibias told you about. It is the subconscious-self's striving for individuality. As such, it is only linked to the spirit of this life; and not your soul. The Ego is only the illusion of individuality." Pan looked closely at Lutrin's positive reaction and asked, "Why ask me this, and not Tibias?"

"Well, he means well, and I'm sure he believes it himself. But ... well ... er."

"Who is not getting to the point now?" demanded Pan, glaring at Lutrin.

"I do not think Tibias, or Thoth either, are exactly who they think they are."

"Not everyone can be 'exactly'; with certainty," replied Pan, "because certainty of belief can be the cause of much suffering."

"Yes, but only certainty in the illusion."

"You have finally surpassed your guide."

Chapter 9: **HALLS of the FREE**

The summer following their trip to see Tibias, Taesus visited Lutrin whilst Aniel was visiting Lucknow. The Gap had gone full circle and the whole Taezali tribe were gathered for the end of summer celebrations. To the surprise of all, Deedle and Tilli were seen walking towards the tree of Brude.

"Although unexpected, welcome my friends," exclaimed a surprised Brude, "no bad news I hope?"

"None, but possible good news that can wait until another time." Deedle was clearly anxious to say why he had come, but seemed a little hesitant.

"In your own time then," said Brude diplomatically.

"We have come to remind you and Aniel that, during the passing of the Doggertaes through these lands, we had discussed establishing a neutral territory. It was to be a place where all the free folk could meet. I hear that Taesus has already set up a dwelling for himself." Although Deedle had voiced this point, Brude sensed that it was just a prelude to something more pressing on the Gridoler's mind.

"Have no fear that you will ever be left behind," replied Brude, "Taesus is to be given a house built by Lutrin, after Lutrin has settled near to Athelney. Until then, nothing has been done to further realise those ideas."

"Perhaps we should start now," said Aniel, "I too was going to speak of this matter."

"What do you suggest?" asked Taesus.

"Initially, the building of a great hall."

"The Halls of the Free," suggested Malceni.

"Why not?" said Brude. "That has a good feel to it. We have so many people here that temporary dwellings could be completed in days. And when it is done, the first point on the agenda shall be your 'good news' Deedle." Deedle was grateful that Brude knew that there was something else he wanted to say. "I must add however, that no final place can be agreed upon yet."

"Thank you," Deedle said, bowing low and retreating to a food laden table.

The evening was full of song and dance, and reminded Malceni a little of their time in Belevedon.

*

Brude was, as ever, true to his word. A week later, a large mead-hall, with ante-chambers leading off it, was erected on a small hill overlooking the lake. One chamber was allocated to each of the free people. In addition, a number of huts were also built to house visiting guests. Plans were made for a great feast and the exchanging of gifts.

Before the feast, when all were assembled, Brude called upon Deedle to speak. Like all those present, Deedle was in his finest clothes. He raised himself to his full height and said, "The news I have is relevant to the gift giving. We Gridolers have come to offer a gift to your people Aniel, in the hope that should you grant my request, the granting will be as your gift to us."

"Deedle," began Aniel, "I truly am not being obstructive, but this does not sound like a gift. It appears to be more of an exchange that you desire."

"Let this be the first step in understanding each others' culture then. We Gridolers treat such exchanges as gift giving. It is the only way we know to transcend our laws of construction. You see, when a Gridoler 'sells' anything it is really only 'on loan,' so to speak, until the receiver dies. I am unable to explain it further in the Babel tongue."

Aniel could see that Deedle was being sincere, and that his attempts to explain it were a source of discomfort. However, before he could offer a word of understanding, Tarquin said, "Then teach us your tongue, that we may know more of your race."

"That can never be. I am sorry. We did not mean to cause offence. Come Tilli." The Gridolers made ready to leave.

"No," said Aniel, "do not go. Tarquin is only showing his own curiosity. That is a Finnic trait that your race needs to understand. Come, I will not take offence. What exchange of gifts would you like to give?"

Deedle appeared reticent. "The matter relates to our spiritual home, although we have only just learnt that it was not actually where we originated from."

"Of what place do you speak?" asked Brude.

"It is the Shivering Mountain. We would like to live there. But the Finns chased us out."

"I see," said Aniel carefully, "we know that it was not your home or we would not have done so."

"But why do you wish to keep it from us?" Tilli blurted out unceremoniously.

Aniel went to speak, but Tarquin interjected, "It is not permitted to speak of our reason."

"I see that Deedle and I have hasty companions in common". Tarquin and Tilli looked a little uneasy. "Tarquin," said Aniel smiling, "was it not I who made that rule, long before your arrival here?" Tarquin nodded and Aniel continued, "When Finns first came to Belevedon, Mam Tor, or Moon Tor as we called it, was the site of an ancient tree of light. It has been said of old that there was a door, a door that is 'magic' by human understanding. The door is an instant gateway across the great lake and out onto AnTara, the site of a second tree of light, that which gave Sunna its name. Were we to discover it, we could have easier access, in times of haste, to Portowest. We have been looking for the door. This is why we keep it."

"Then I will shed more light on this matter," said Deedle. "For we know where the door is."

"And you would tell us?" asked Tarquin.

"It would do you no good. It is a Gridoler door. Only Gridolers can enter."

"But you said that you did not originally come from there."

"That is so, but it is the door to our origins. We dwelt in AnTara. A wizard cast an enchantment on us, causing us to sleep for an Age. When we awoke we remembered nothing and none of us had aged a day. Only now does the full effect of his spell seem to be wearing off. So much so that I can now put a face to this wizard."

"But that land was given to the Doggertaes," said Taesus. "War would come if a Gridolish host went there now."

"Because of the Firbolg prophecy, AnTara itself was not given to your people," Brude reminded Taesus.

"What prophecy is this?" asked Taesus,

"That one day the AnTara range would be laid waste by greedy and selfish men. As a shadow of itself, Ru would become known as Urru."

"I am trying to avert a disaster by asking for something that we can accept instead. Would any other race here do likewise?" No one spoke. "My point has been made, but I will say more in the hope of answering the unasked question. The faults, in the mountain we were forced into, were not of our making, as Brude once suspected and I admit I wasn't sure myself until recently, but rather it is the result of earth tremors. They were the prelude, warnings if you like, to the great quake that engulfed Dogger."

"In truth Deedle," said Aniel, "I did not know that I was sending you somewhere unpleasant. Our rouse was planned carefully. We thought that you only wanted the Vasa Murrhina, so we guided you to the end of the seam."

'What is Vasa Murrhina? thought Malceni to Lutrin.

'It is Blue-John.'

'What is Blue-John?' asked Malceni mentally.

'Not sure, what it is.'

"Give my head peace," grumbled Taesus.

"Shush, you three," commanded Brude trying to concentrate on Aniel's words, "Where were we? Oh yes, I thought as much, did I not say so Deedle?"

"Yes, which is why I say we are being more than understanding."

"Stay Deedle," said Aniel, "and tell us what you wanted to give my people."

"You can never use the door and, although it is not 'magic' or as instant as you'd like, we have dug you a tunnel underneath the sea. A tunnel that emerges only a few hundred yards from here. We have also nearly finished a tunnel that follows the Blue-John seam all the way to Mam Tor."

There were gasps of astonishment from the assembly, but Tarquin was quick to remark, "A fine achievement, but it would take just as long to walk through that as it would to cross the Ridge."

Meanwhile, no one in the Hall had heard the beating of mighty wings, the shadow cast across the lake or a tall man now listening at the doorway. "What Tarquin says is true," said Amergin, striding into the hall, "as long as there is a Ridge to cross."

Taesus was out of his chair, knife in hand. "Thoth," he shouted. "Bring him down Deedle and I will kill him."

"The wizard's face," snarled Deedle, pulling out his short sword. The floor-boards shuddered as they all rose to their feet.

"It must be him," said Aniel. "We know that he walks abroad and Amergin does not."

Perhaps Thoth's moment of compassion would have brought about what he'd desired all along, if it hadn't have been for Lutrin stepping forward in time to stop the onslaught.

"Wait," he commanded. "Lest you murder an innocent hall-watcher."

"What more proof do you need?" shouted Tilli.

"Who can determine his true nature?" called another voice from the back of the crowd. It was Pan.

Lutrin grinned, "I suspect that you might be standing in my place had I not stepped forward."

"If I could, perhaps," replied Pan. "Now show us what you've learnt."

"Look at me," Lutrin said to the wizard. "Look me straight in the eye and tell me who you are."

Lutrin stared into those cold grey eyes. "I am Amergin, youngest of the five, enemy of Thoth."

"Miserable trickster," shouted Tilli.

"He speaks the truth," said Lutrin, with a sigh of relief.

"How do you know?"

"The answer is in his eyes. However, although he is Amergin, that does not mean he is not dangerous. He has a story to tell I think. A story that can wait until after Deedle and Aniel have dealt with the outcomes resulting from important parley. Until then ... ," he stopped and held out his hand, "... your staff please Master Amergin. No one here will hurt you, unless they want to dishonour the laws of hospitality." Amergin nodded and passed his staff to Lutrin.

"Continue," said Brude to Aniel.

"Amergin is correct," said Aniel. "We should be grateful for this gift one day. Deedle, I will accept this gift on one condition. Show us that we can not transcend the door of Mam Tor and the mountain will be returned to you."

"We are leaving Tilli. My word was my bond."

"Then twice I say stay. We have an agreement. May I request that you Deedle, newly appointed King of Mam Tor, show me the door at your convenience."

A great cheer went up from all the free folk. Many got up and patted Deedle and Tilli on the back. "Thank you. Many thanks to all the Finns and Elfin. All the more do I relish mentioning the rest of the gift." Silence fell across the floor. The atmosphere had been charged so much that it had not yet dissipated with the cheers.

"Nay, do not worry. Just this. The new tunnel is quicker than just walking. The Finns need not walk if they don't want to. We have built a track on which a carriage can move on wheels. The carriage is pulled along by a series of weights and pulleys."

"Is there no end to Gridolish ingenuity?" laughed Taesus.

When the cheers and applause had subsided, Malceni turned to Tilli. "Do you have a different name for small Gridolers. You know, much smaller than yourselves?"

"Only for our children, the Griduini. We pride ourselves on not judging character by size."

"I think the feast should begin," said Brude, "Aniel, Deedle, Lutrin, Taesus and I will talk with Amergin. You are also welcome Pan. It would be an injustice to openly humiliate Amergin in such a large group." They went off to a table quietly. It was there that Amergin told them of his plight and possession by Thoth, followed by his release and escape.

"What happened to Garaldina and the two faeries?" asked Lutrin.

"Of the faery that fell, I know not. As for the others, they are living in a little house I built on the Shivering Mountain."

"Is there any token by which we might accept that you are fully free of Thoth?" asked Taesus.

"Possibly. Lutrin, do you have your mirror with you?"

"I gave it away to Malceni."

"Please ask him to bring it here."

Lutrin called Malceni over. "Here it is," he said, handing it to Amergin.

"No. You have a look."

"At what?"

"The handle. Unscrew the handle." Malceni obliged and, in doing so, pulled out a knife. "Taesus," Amergin went on, "please take out your knife." Taesus obliged. "The knife that you have Malceni is the one that can kill Thoth. The one that you have Taesus is the one that can kill me. Had you simply scratched my skin then Amergin would have died. At that moment, Thoth would have became physical once more in my body. Not knowing where the other knife was you could not have defeated him. He would have slaughtered you all."

"Okay," said Malceni, "I get the point."

"May I?" Amergin reached for his staff.

Chapter 10: The BATTLE

Assembled in the Halls of the Free were Taesus, Aniel, Tarquin, Brude, Malceni, Amergin, Deedle, Tilli, Lutrin, Lucknow, Pan, Volas and the Woodwose. Perched on a stand opposite Aniel was Black-Back, Lord of the Gulls. Tilli kept his distance from the Gull, which was one of the few animals that he did not like; for he considered them to be cruel creatures. The Roc was outside, lying on the ground with her head just inside the main doorway. It was Brude who spoke first, "With great sadness we gather today. War is almost upon us and we should coordinate our efforts. This could be our final gathering, so all should report as best they can."

Pan stood to speak, "I will act when I can. But remember, you can not always rely upon me. I must only intervene when I consider important elements of nature to be threatened. Quite possibly anyone here might also see my wrath." He looked at Amergin from the corner of his eye, "So please, act carefully."

"In war, one acts instinctively," retorted Amergin irritably.

"As do I," replied Pan. He spoke quietly, but there was a menacing undertone.

"Please do not argue," pleaded Lucknow. The Gridolers wondered who she thought was arguing.

"This is not a discussion for females," said Deedle.

"If it takes a female to remind friends not to argue," said Volas quite calmly, "then clearly it is wiser to include us. Norbold would be delighted to see it otherwise."

Amergin saw that Lucknow was wearing Lutrin's pendant.

"Lutrin, you must wear your pendant in battle."

"Why?"

"There is something I should tell you. And the whole truth I will not reveal until the war is over. The pendant was made by Thoth."

"You knew this and yet continued to let me wear it?"

"Yes, and I swore Garaldina to secrecy".

"Never trust a wizard," muttered Deedle.

Amergin ignored him, "It is charmed Lutrin. Thoth wants you to survive the battle."

"For what purpose?"

"So he can torment you with certain knowledge he has."

"Knowledge that you have also I presume," said Malceni.

"Yes," snapped Amergin, "and I will tell you at the end. For now it is sufficient for you to know that the pendant will protect you from harm."

"Then I thank you for the information," said Lutrin, "all the more reason for Lucknow to wear it."

Amergin dropped the subject.

"The Woodwose will speak," said Brude.

"May I translate?" asked Malceni.

"There is no need," boomed the Woodwose, this time in a deep, throaty tone, "Pan has taught me your Babel tongue. The Orci have been laying large barrels along the perimeter of the Tajem forest in the northern territory. I do not know what is in them, but I suspect it can only have a dreadful purpose. A disembodied apparition of Thoth is advising them where to place the barrels."

"I know his mind," said Amergin.

"Too much for my liking," Deedle whispered to Tilli.

"They were designed to blow up and create a fireball," continued Amergin, "not even the Tajem will survive. All will burn."

Tears rolled down the Woodwose's face. "They are almost as old as me," he said, "they were my idea. I created them."

"Perhaps we can save some?" said Tilli anxiously.

"I am sorry Tilli," said Amergin, "but when the fire takes hold, all will burn."

All those present felt very sad for the Woodwose. Pan attempted to cheer him up. "My dear friend," he said to the Woodwose, "I will be sorry for your loss. We all are. Yes, the Tajem trees will be gone but I have been cultivating their seed and have created a fragrant leaf from them."

"I know of this leaf," scoffed Taesus, " and this is all very well, but we must agree on what to do. Fecir has been training and preparing the Doggertaes, so my people at least are doing something."

"Men behave in accordance to their fashion," said Brude, "and Picts according to theirs. We have positioned our warriors in the north-east of Sunna. Aniel has sent a troop of Finni to the Tyne and Deedle will guard all the non-combatants in this area. That will include Lutrin and Malceni."

"I am surprised Lutrin," said Taesus, "I never thought that my friend would hide amongst the maidens."

Although Taesus was only jesting, Lutrin felt a need to respond, "I have a feeling that great danger lurks nearby. Besides, most leaders are with their own people, why should I be any different?"

Aniel was next to speak, "What plans do you have Deedle?"

"We have set up a rolling stone from inside the Western route we gave to your people. If life is threatened, the Picts and Elfin can retreat into the tunnel. Nothing will be able to enter."

Brude lifted a huge cup into the air. "If nothing more is to be said then let us all drink from the battle cup. This may be the last sup we sip together. If it is to be so then let it be as the warriors of old supped."

Just as the last of them shared the cup, all the company heard a loud boom and rushed outside. Far into the north-east they saw the sky all aflame.

"The Tajem will be burning", said Amergin, "and the Ravens are gathering. War is upon us. But, for what it is worth, the Orci can not succeed against our alliance. Nonetheless, they will destroy many beautiful things."

*

Fecir's men fought long and hard and may have lost their battle had it not been for a small number of Picts who helped them. The Picts were armed with a Tajem branch each. They darted around the enemy, thrashed as many Orci as they could and then retreated back into the forest.

"Battle-dodgers," shouted Fecir, "tail-turning forest rats."

An old Pict went back to the melee and stood before Fecir. 'Fecir you?' he thought and, realising he wasn't speaking, "You Fecir?" he asked.

"I don't like your tone little Pict, allies or not I might give you a kick up the backside."

"Just keep the Orci at bay for an hour. Do not attack yet. Keep your losses down. After an hour, then go on the attack."

Fecir gave him a puzzled look.

"They are Tajem branches Master Fecir."

Realising his mistake, Fecir knelt and looked the Pict in the eye, "My apologies."

"Retreat," ordered Fecir, "back inside the fort of Bodhun."

In less than an hour, over half of the Orci lay dead or dying. Fecir enjoyed finishing off the rest. However, just as victory was at hand, a large black cloud came heading in their direction and the heat became intense. Soon the whole area would be engulfed in smoke. They would all die in the wael-rec.

*

In the north-east, the Picts had little to do. They sat around trying to be cheerful. None of them had participated in battle before. At least they knew that their families were safe and that their animals had been moved south. No Orci had been seen, but then a great black cloud headed their way. The whole Tajem forest was bursting into flame and the smoke threatened everyone. Worse still, the fire was unnatural. It was so hot that it melted even the stones.

After this report from the Gulls, Amergin called on the Roc. Within a few minutes he found himself in the centre of the Eyribol Ridge.

He took a deep breath and began chanting, " Clem shelac mac agal oshanto. Clem shelac mac agal oshanto," over and over again; and the light shining from his staff grew ever brighter. The wind began to strengthen in speed and volume. Amergin continued chanting. Some of the water from the lake was thrown into the air, creating superheated steam. Amergin continued still. The wind ripped up burning Tajems and sent them hurtling north. A combination of the steam and trees hitting the already fragile ice-cap sent shock-waves through the ice, but still the ice held back the sea.

Amergin could do no more, so he and the Roc headed for Manni. It was time to face Thoth.

*

Pan meanwhile, was self-incarnating on top of the ice-cap.

*

As the wind died down, the Orci war-band burst into Sunna from the northern territory. The Picts, being taken by surprise, ran into the charred forest and, using their special Pictish magic, they 'became as stone'. The Orci made their way to the lake shoreline and examined their prize.

"Wur father will have a fight on his hands," said a warrior, "if he thinks I'm going to give this land to 'im."

"Surely yow meant to say 'wae' brother, not 'I'?" said another, rather slyly.

"Aye, of course," replied the first brother.

"I wonder what Pictish woman are like?"

"As hard as rock I hear. Best to drive the lot of 'em oot and send for wur own lasses".

"Aye. Aye. What's the first thing yow will do when wae've dealt with father?"

"Cut up that servant of his. He's too influential on 'im; mad' 'im soft."

"Yer reet. He did dat; mad' 'im soft all reet. And he got 'im hooked on the leaf".

"Come on, let's get some grub. I'm starvin'."

*

It was at this time that Brude realised that the battle was really all about glory for Norbold. Most of what was happening up north was just a rouse, a decoy. A group of Orci had sailed all the way to Portowest and had made their way along the Finnic road through the oak forest. Norbold was with them. They saw Brude in a clearing talking to the faeries. The Orci grabbed, gagged and bound Brude. He hadn't resisted. It was him they were after. "Yow will look good as a blood eagle," said Norbold gloating. He told two men to guard him whilst the rest went on.

*

"Hide, run," shouted a small Elf running towards the Hall of the Free. Aniel was there. He took the Elf by the hand and hid in a secret anti-chamber. It was then that he realised that the Gridolers had not finished digging the adjoining tunnel that led to the Western route. They could hear the Orci outside and remained quiet.

Lutrin turned to Volas, "Quickly, take the maidens to the Gridoler tunnel. Together with the Gridolers, I shall try to hold them off."

They all ran as fast as they could towards the tunnel.

Taesus, Tarquin and Malceni were examining the Western route and hadn't heard the shout that the Orci had arrived. As the others came piling into the tunnel they became accidentally trapped because Tilli rolled the stone over the passage way. The chain mechanism had not been tested yet and broke; locking them in the tunnel. It would take time to open the door by hand.

*

The Gridolers fought with stout-hearts, and were holding their own against the Orci. Lutrin projected his tura around the enemy. He gave them images of a wild Pan facing them. This caused many of them to panic and flee back into the forest, where the angry Woodwose was waiting for them.

Norbold would have been taken if it hadn't have been for his battle Shaman. The Shaman threw out a gaseous cloud that knocked out the Gridolers. Lutrin was at the mercy of Norbold.

*

"Get the door open!" shouted Lucknow. "I will not hide in here during a battle!"

"But Lutrin ordered us to stay my lady," cried an Elf maiden.

"I may be a small Elf, but I am still the daughter of one of the ancient Finni. I take orders from no one. Bar the way again, unless some of you would rather die fighting than be left to the mercy of the Orci when the battle is over. They would do despicable things to those who survive."

"I'm with you," said Titch.

Taesus, Tarquin and Malceni were shouting from the back of the crowd, but they could not be heard over the masses.

Enough of the stone was pushed back for Lucknow to get out. She would not be alone. Slowly, one by one, the others emerged with little daggers in their hands. By the time Taesus, Tarquin and Malceni got out, they did not know where the action was. They separated. Malceni was seen heading for the lake with only one thing on his mind.

*

Lucknow saw Lutrin in deadly combat with Norbold. 'My poor Lu,' she thought, 'it would break his heart if he had to take a life deliberately.'

Lutrin was too busy to see where that thought had come from, but he felt Lucknow's presence nearby. Being no match for an Orci warrior, Lutrin couldn't hold out for long.

"This is the end. Al gut yow like a fish yow deformed squirrel," bellowed Norbold.

Lutrin could smell Norbold's foul breath "Strike me down and you will make me powerful. I will reincarnate as a Roc and swallow your fat head."

"With Naegling in my hand, Nin of your rattish magic scares me," laughed Norbold, who felt victory was at hand.

"Lutrin!" screamed Lucknow.

He looked over at her, smiled, and thought, 'I love you' and whispered, "Goodbye." He held up his hand to wave.

"Catch this."

Lutrin realised that Lucknow had thrown him the Panara pendant. It was well aimed. The Pendant was in Lutrin's hand just as Norbold brought his sword down towards Lutrin's head. Nothing happened. The sword stopped inches from his head. Lutrin put the pendant around his neck but, having been altered to fit Lucknow, it was now a tight fit. However, using the palm of his hand the Orci battle Shaman began searching for the energy shield's achilles heel. His eyes lit up when he found it and directed his own energy through the palm of his hand to a particular spot near Lutrin. Norbold knew what the smile meant. He stepped forward and kicked the feet from under Lutrin, who now lay flat on his back.

"Al remove your head with wun blow."

This truly was the end. No one was near to save him. No friends around to help. No Roc bird in the sky. 'It was not meant to be like this,' thought Lutrin.

Aniel left the Halls of the Free and headed towards the melee. He saw Lucknow rushing forward.

The Shaman thrust a knife into Lucknow's side. She crumpled to the floor and her eyes glazed over. As they did so, Lutrin saw a streak of light burst forth from her eyes. The light turned and headed towards the north-west and over the horizon. She was gone. Lutrin lay there and didn't even struggle.

Brude had easily escaped from his captors. He 'became as stone' and the ropes had fell from him. His guards ran off into the oak forest, where they too met the Woodwose. Brude came running towards Norbold, shouting, "death, death." But he was too late. The sword came down upon Lutrin's neck.

*

Pan had to intervene. He stamped on the ice. The ice-cap could no longer take the pressure of the sea. It collapsed into the great lake, creating a tidal wave that grew as the sea behind the wave magnified its height. Pan fell onto a hard rock. He looked up as millions of tons of ice blocks came crashing towards him. 'Oh dear,' he thought, 'I don't think I can die ... can I?' He was engulfed by the weight, and saw no more. Black-Back was there to see him fall.

*

Malceni meanwhile, having possession of the knife from Lutrin's mirror, was determined to kill Thoth. He had watched Lutrin closely and knew enough to learn how to open a bridge to Manni. Believing Thoth to be distracted by the fire, wind and water, Malceni crept into the castle. He made his way into the northern most room, over-looking the lake, and saw the apparition of Thoth standing there.

"I am proud of you," said Thoth, "you have come to murder me in my own home, you wicked little Pict."

"Nothing more than a dark-harrower deserves."

"It will eat away at you if you kill me. Oh, and you are so worthy to deal out death are you not? Even I have not given myself such an honour."

"That is because you are a coward. You get others to kill for you."

"If I could, I'd make an exception in your case," grinned Thoth.

"Let's get this over with," said Malceni walking towards him.

"You would kill me before even hearing me out," Thoth said, feigning surprise and clutching his hands to his breast.

Malceni walked to the window and placed the knife on the ledge. "I'm listening."

"Look behind you."

"Oh come on, I'm not that stupid."

"I have no body. I can not hurt you. Look behind you."

As Malceni looked, his face went white with terror. "Oh ..."

"You may have time to escape. Run."

Malceni ran outside the door and stopped to go back for the knife. He felt the rush of wind on his face and ran. Luck was with him. The rushing wind was the Roc bird. The Roc grabbed him and flew straight up. He couldn't see him, but on the back of the Roc was Amergin. The wizard diverted some of the burning Tajem towards the castle.

The burning logs landed next to Thoth. He felt no danger, but, for a moment, he felt lonely. 'Perhaps it might be nice to go home,' he thought, 'things haven't exactly turned out right for me.' The wind was howling through the room as the wave finally hit the castle. As the water hit the window, the knife left by Malceni went spinning through the air.

Thoth was struck by the realisation that the metal, combined with the wind, fire and water had somehow penetrated his spirit. He did not scream or shout with anger. Amergin could hear Thoth say peacefully, "Arh ... it is done."

*

The wave was now so powerful that much of the lake's waters were sucked back into it, revealing the bottom of the lake bed in front of the Eyribol Ridge. The whole Ridge shuddered and cracked as the wave struck it. It too was finished. The Ridge collapsed and island of Ru was formed; but so too in the north-west were the islands of Malaius, Scetis and Dumma uncovered. However, the large Island had been split into two; and the Ru Sea ran between the two large islands. The great lake was gone, as was all of its shoreline. All the tree homes were destroyed, but so too were all of the Orci warriors who had gathered by the great lake.

*

Fecir's people realised they were safe now, as did the Picts who had 'become as stone'.

*

There was an almighty bang as the sword struck Lutrin's neck. But it wasn't the blast that knocked Norbold onto his back unconscious. It was a horse's hoof. The sword had hit the pendant and cracked open the time vortex. Panara burst forth and kicked Norbold in the face. The Shaman was quick. Lutrin had no time to thank Panara because the Shaman stuck his knife into her. Brude was there just in time to kill the Shaman before he could get to Lutrin.

"It's been a long time little Lu," choked Panara. A little blood dripped from the side of her mouth.

"Dematerialise Panara. Go back to own dimension and regenerate," said Lutrin.

"No. This is it. You see, Thoth took my physical form from my own dimension. I'm dying. But, oh, to see your face one last time; my Lu," She coughed a little more blood.

"I did not know," he said with tears in his eyes. A gentle breeze drifted by him and, briefly, he caught the scent of her hair.

"I want to become a person. Will the Gap take me?"

"I don't know. I just don't know."

"I think that I do," she said. A mist-filled light rose up from Panara's chest and drifted over the ground, coming to rest on Lucknow.

"No," said Lutrin, "Lucknow is gone."

Lutrin heard the words, 'I know.'

With what seemed like raucous glee, a gull was heard overhead, screeching, "Pan is dead." Brude lowered his head and wept.

Aniel came running to Lucknow. Not far away, the Roc landed with Amergin and Malceni. Taesus and Tarquin came running back also.

Aniel kissed both of Lucknow's eyes and was about to lay her back down again when he felt a tingling sensation in the palm of his left hand. 'But I saw her light depart for the place of waiting,' he thought.

After whispering words of enchantment, he breathed life back into her and put his palm upon her wound. It began to close up, but not completely.

"That is far enough Aniel. Do not kill yourself as well," said Tarquin, pulling Aniel's hand away. As Aniel stood they could see blood dripping from his side. "He has taken some of the wound upon himself," said Tarquin, "but now Lucknow shall live."

As Lucknow regained consciousness, the first sight she saw was Lutrin. "Lucknow," he asked.

"Yes, and no."

"What is this?" exclaimed Brude.

"The immortal element of Lucknow has indeed gone to be with her ancestors" she replied. "However, her spirit is here and has merged as one with Panara's soul."

"Incredible," said Aniel. "An Elf with both a soul and a spirit. It is ... it's just not possible."

'Pan is dead,' was the thought now in all the Picts and Elfin minds.

"Long live Pan", shouted Pan, arriving somewhat late to the scene. "I suppose all things are possible in the Bryhery Gap," he said dreamily.

"We are not in the Gap at the moment," said Brude, both delighted to see him, but also feeling embarrassed at his tears, "did you have a hand in all of this?" The Finns weren't sure who Brude was talking to.

"Actually, it was both of us," said Amergin, who was walking up behind Pan, "we both acted 'instinctively' today." Aniel saw Pan's shadow cast upon the ground.

"As such, we haven't broken any rules have we," mused a smiling Pan.

They were all too busy to notice that Norbold had regained consciousness and had stood up, collecting his sword. Fortunately, the Roc bird, paying no heed to the group of people standing around, saw Norbold and decided that she must be hungry. Except for his hand, that still grasped Naegling*, Norbold was never seen again.

The Woodwose finally returned from the oak forest. Pan gave him a hearty pat on the back. "It is a very nice wood isn't it Woodwose." He nodded. "It needs a lot of looking after. I don't suppose .... ?"

"Listen," his voice boomed in response, "it is time for me to leave." The Woodwose sat down and closed his eyes. The others gathered around him. "Be seeing you," he said, "very soon."

The faery lights surrounded him and became so bright that they had to look away. On looking back they saw a tall handsome oak tree floating into the forest. "I was a Tajem Woodwose for a long time," he shouted, "I think I will enjoy seeing what being an oak Woodwose is like."

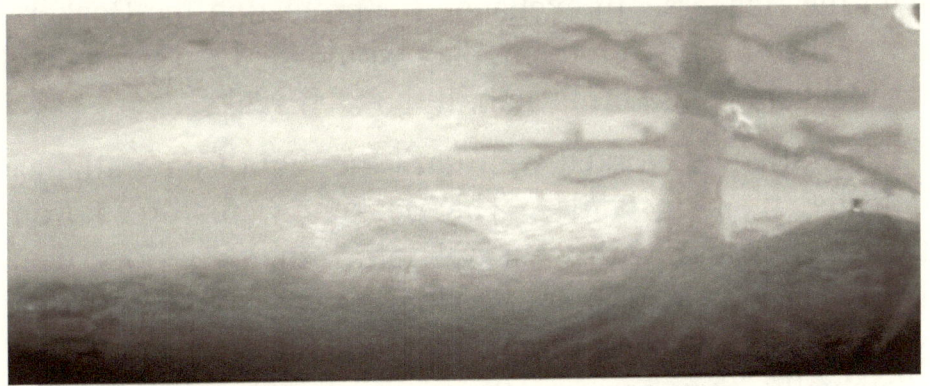

At the Gridolers' request, this grisly trophy was later hung above the doorway of the Great Hall.

Chapter 11: The ORCI

Orcades was a bleak and dismal place. To the east lay a mountain of ice stretching for hundreds of miles to the far northern lands; and from that north came a biting wind. In the distant past the Orci, which was a combination of two tribes, had made a perilous journey across a frozen wilderness.

One clan, of settled farmers and pottery makers, came from so far in the south-east of the world that few would even guess where from anymore. Known as the Beaker folk in those days, they came under increasing attacks from people whom they had once traded with. And so, an unusual union was formed with a tribe of vicious warriors. Now part of a new movement of Celts, they were shunned by other Celts for their lack of compassion. This made them even more violent, so much so that eventually they had no place to rest during the winter months. Then they acquired a new leader who had originated from the Beaker folk. This leader persuaded his clan to form an alliance with the Beakers. In exchange for protecting the Beakers, rather than destroying them, they would be the warriors and the Beakers would bring stability to their ranks.

This alliance worked well until the main Celtic alliance defeated them in battle. The Beakers were forced from their homes and, with what was left of their warriors, went in search of a new home. Along the way their warriors were joined by Norn stragglers from the Vericones tribe. Eventually, they came to the frozen lands and from there they were forced to attempt a journey into the unknown.

When all seemed lost, a wizard appeared before them and helped them to survive. His name was Thoth. Thoth had lied to them though. He told them to keep going north before heading west. If they had gone west beforehand, they would have come to northern Dogger, which was unoccupied at that time.

Their spoken tongue was a mixture of Angle, Jute, Norn and what would one day be known as Saxon, with much of the eastern Beaker words long lost. At first they had to learn new skills. They dug out the earth, made homes of stone where they had dug, and then covered them with earth again. Beaker skills gave the homes a civilised feeling, but the need for fighting skills was much greater. Many wild animals and giant white bears saw the Orci as food. As such, it took many years to hunt down and destroy all the bears.

Gradually, the seasons got warmer and they were able to control their environment to the extent that talk of gaining a better land took place. Scouts were sent to the south. They reported that the animals needed controlling before the whole tribe could move on. And so it was that the Orci took many an age to eliminate all but the most elusive of animals that could destroy them. More scouts were sent and many died when they tried to get through an impenetrable wall of trees.

The wizard of legend returned to them and promised to one day help them take the rest of the land. He gave power to the bad Shamans who used it to eliminate the good ones. The healers were gone, replaced by those immersed in the dark arts of Thoth. However, throughout the whole of Orci history, there existed a secret society known as the Brotherhood.

The Brotherhood's aim was to stay hidden until they could take power and lead the tribe back to its peaceful and spiritual roots. Their first leader was known as Mithras. Mithras had told them the time would be right when they heard Thoth speak of his brother, Mergin.

The Orci, still small in number, found it necessary to trade with a new group of people called the Doggi. Unbeknownst to both, the Orci and Doggi were related through their joint Baltic, Anglo-Saxon and Celtic stock. The Doggi lived in the far south-east, on Doggerbank. As the temperatures rose, part of Orcades was now open to a newly formed sea route. Many battles went unresolved with the Doggi, until a truce was formed where each would leave the other alone, if neither interfered with the other. Thoth now believed that the time was right to make his move and use the Orci to help him. He returned to Orcades to talk with Norbold, the Jarl of Orcades. Meanwhile, the Brotherhood began to sense that their time was drawing near.

****

Umov the 'Slick' began serving Norbold a seal steak during his conversation with Thoth. Tall, short-haired and clean-shaven, Umov was always attentive to Norbold's wishes and plans.

"So, yow brother a A..mergin," said Norbold, stumbling over the pronunciation, "is against us. And he also looks like yow?" Norbold was trying his best to talk in a way that Thoth could understand him. In battle, Norbold was less comprehensible. Umov's green eyes widened and his ears twitched.

Thoth sat back in his chair close to the large fireplace in Norbold's stone-roofed barrow. Considering his rank, it was a very small and cosy place. But Norbold wanted it so; why have something cold and draughty just to look important? "That is right," said Thoth. "Originally, all of my brothers, including Mithras, looked similar. It was only when we went our separate ways and developed our individuality that we started to differ." Umov almost tripped over the dog that was sleeping in front of the fire. The dog jumped and growled.

"Watch it Umov, a good hunting dog is worth far more than yow sorry neck," grizzled Norbold.

"He might catch your meat, but no one could cook it quite like me," smiled Umov.

"Get me some Dogger ale, and don't push yow luck." Norbold didn't mean it. There was no chance he would get rid of Umov.

"You drank all we had," scolded Umov, "and the new shipment hasn't arrived yet. I'm afraid there is only Pictish heather ale. The old batch which you got from Fecir."

"That Fecir," he said, "overcharging for a barrel of Pictish muck."

"It was a young ale then. At this point it is probably better than the Doggi's batch."

"He is probably right," said Thoth, "you call them both ale. And yet the Picts' brew is more of a wine. Ale can go off, whereas the wine will mature."

Norbold sat silently until Umov returned.

"Yuck," said Norbold, although he actually liked it, "it tastes like cow dung." Umov teasingly went to remove it.

"No, leave it. It'll do." Umov went to leave. "No, stay. There are few I can trust to do anything reet anymore."

Before sitting down, Umov poured himself a drink, but then stood up again. "Before I sit, shall I get you some pipe-leaf. I understand it is very good for you."

"Aye. Yow are a good servant after all."

Thoth stared suspiciously at Umov as he left the room. "I'm not so sure about him. The leaf can bring about a slow death in humans."

"He is loyal. He once jumped in front of a spear for me. Assassination attempts are an occupational hazard in Orcades. Another time, he took a knife. Watch this when he comes back."

Umov returned with the pipe and leaf.

"Thoth here thinks yow want me dead," said Norbold, trying to look serious.

"Why would I want that? I come off very well in this relationship. If anyone in this room does not have my master's interests at heart it is a conniving old wizard."

Thoth went to react, but Norbold stayed his hand and started laughing. "See. He is also honest, even to the point of death." He signaled for them both to sit down.

Both Norbold and Thoth noticed that Umov lit a pipe and breathed the leaf in deeply. "What's good for the goose eh?" he said smiling.

"Let us get on with the business at hand. Why are yow here Thoth?" asked Norbold.

Thoth was about to speak when a particularly large cloud of leaf aroma from Umov floated past. As it did so, Thoth coughed and, just for a moment, seemed to lose concentration. Umov could swear that he thought the wizard's eyes changed colour for a moment.

Norbold didn't notice the eyes, but laughed again, "Dear me. Thousands of years old and yow canna cope with a little pipe-leaf."

"I am fine. I had a long journey, that's all."

"Well go on then," said Norbold, clearly enjoying Thoth's discomfort.

"It is time. Time to move against the Islanders."

"Why now?" Norbold had a suspicious nature, which is why he was still alive.

"Because you will need my help. But my brother is fighting me. You need to strike now to be certain of my help."

"So, we both need each other."

Thoth felt grizzly at acknowledging this fact and decided to change the subject. "A more urgent matter is at hand. The Picts are evolving and one amongst them in particular needs to be either killed or taken under your guidance."

"Is this the one that the battle Shaman saw in the runes when you were last here?" asked Umov.

"The same."

"And his name?" Asked Norbold.

"Lutrin. Believe me, he could either destroy you or help you become Lord of all the Island. I shall make arrangements to ensure he comes within your reach.

But remember, if anything goes wrong I must still appear to be helping them and not you."

"I understand why yow behave so. But to me it is a dishonourable way to live." He went to spit, but swallowed it instead when Umov gave him a dirty look.

"Do not tell me that you are developing compassion Norbold?"

"I have compassion, but wur culture is one of war. Wae deal in death, and I canna afford to look weak. Wae are what wae are because others have made us so. Besides, in battle, a madness takes me. When the 'Trumpa creda' horn sounds, I feel a power operating through me."

'Yes,' thought Thoth, 'it is I who live through you. Few realise that if someone lives their life through another, they are a vampire living off the energy of the other person.' "If you are compassionate," said Thoth, "why do you perform the blood eagle ritual on your enemies?"

"As yow call it, it is a ritual. But it is only performed on enemy leaders. Yow were not the only being to visit my ancestors when wae crossed the northern land of ice." Norbold grinned because he thought that he was getting the better hand of the night's discussion.

Thoth pretended to be interested in the story. What Norbold didn't know was that the being he would name was actually Thoth in another form. "Please continue," said Thoth.

"A gallows-prince appeared before them. A warrior god called Odin. He taught them many things. But all Gods demand sacrifice, coupled with mercy. When the battle madness leaves us, wae become merciful.

But the vanquished leader must be sacrificed. It is a gruesome and slow death because a leader should die defending his people and not be caught alive." Not looking in Umov's direction, he spat towards the fire, but missed and hit the dog in the eye. It knew better than to growl at Norbold, but obviously thought that it would get no peace tonight, so it sulked off into an adjoining room. "Where are yow off to? Yer big sissy!" The dog ignored him.

***

Some years later, a grey-haired Norbold and Thoth met again. The loyal Umov was, as ever, present.

"My head Thoth," began Norbold, "has two mixed and confusing memories." He was clearly distressed.

"Continue."

"Well, I see two faces for Lutrin, one looks human and the other less so. In one memory, I nearly have 'im but then a darkness befalls me. Again, this time I have 'im but he escapes. During a trade with the Doggi, Fecir told my men that the poika must have drooned."

"It can't be explained in one evening," said Thoth thoughtfully, "but both were real. All the more reason for you to start the attack soon. I am weaker and your enemy gets stronger."

"So, your brother won then?" added Norbold.

"It was Mithras who intervened. I have no bodily form, but the violent elements of nature are under my control."

"The weather," sneered Norbold, "yow're going to defeat my enemies by doin' a rain dance? My battle Shaman could do as much."

"Can he create a wave a thousand feet high? Can he cause the earth to tremble and break apart, or the ice-cap to shatter?" The room had become black. Thoth had sucked all the light from it. The flame in the fire gave off no heat.

"What do yow want me to do?" said Norbold, trying not to look bothered.

"I will give you a list of ingredients. You will get them and mix them in precisely the manner I tell you."

Thoth spoke and Umov took notes. Umov would not intervene. His group was not proactive in bringing about change. Its place was to wait. 'But Mithras,' he thought, when he was out of room getting some refreshments for Norbold, 'mighty Mithras is on the move. Surely our time is drawing near. I must stay close to Norbold.' On joining the discussion again he said, "Master. When you go to battle, I would like to go with you."

"Yow've never lifted a sword in your life. What's up with yow?"

"You are getting old. Someone should watch your back. Your sons are getting restless."

"My sons won't be with me. I'm goin' on a mission, but I'm happy to take yow with me. Al be sure of success and am equally certain that there will be less danger than most battles contain."

"Tell me your plan," asked Thoth.

***

Time passed, and the Orci went to war. Many boats headed for Hronesness and also to Tyne-cave point. Norbold's and Umov's boat had a different destination though.

The boat trip from the Tarvedum peninsula was far more enjoyable than Umov imagined. He didn't realise of course, but Thoth had created favourable sailing conditions for them. However, as they entered Lemannonius bay near Portowest, someone thought they saw a Finnic ship on the horizon.

There was no harbour master present on a Sunday, which ironically was Mithras' day. As such, they made haste into the port and dragged their boat deep into the oak forest.

The battle Shaman, who was dressed as a woman, muttered a few charms and claimed that no one could track them. The warriors believed that a male Shaman dressed as a woman was a very powerful combination of the male and female energies. As such, they feared a male Shaman even more. Any man that could use the female energy within must be extra special.

Although Umov was highly amused, he had to admit that he never knew if this practice, of incorporating the energy of another gender, really worked or not.

They had plenty of time before the war started. Nevertheless, they needed to be in the right place at the right time. Provisions were plentiful, so they started their uneventful walk through the oak forest, along the old Finnic road.

*

The time for attack was near. They heard the explosions and saw the fire in the sky.

Thoth had provided a good description of their target. There he was, in a clearing, talking to some faeries. Umov was delighted to see the faeries, but didn't show it. They captured the Pict and tied him up.

Believing Umov had gone far enough with him, Norbold ordered him and a warrior to stay and guard their prisoner. Umov knew about Pictish stone magic, so he wasn't surprised when the Pict 'became as stone'.

When the warrior ran in fear he pretended to do likewise, but stopped short of going too far into the forest. He was glad that he hadn't, for a few seconds later he heard the sound of a skull being crunched. Whatever creature had been responsible for the noise was now stalking Umov, so he decided to get out into the open as soon as possible.

He was too slow.

The creature did not immediately attack, but eyed him up slowly. Umov removed his sword, cutting his finger as he did so, and placed it on the ground. He didn't know it, but the creature sensed that the sword had never seen battle.

If he was going to die now, he wanted to go out in a manner fitting a member of his order. He removed his shirt, and from his pocket took out an amulet to place around his neck. "You probably don't understand. But thank you beast for waiting. I am ready."

The creature floated towards him. Umov felt his bowels move but managed to control them. "I am a guardian of the hidden truth of Mithras. It is by his grace alone that you can hurt me."

The beast picked up the sword. There was blood on its feet. Umov was nearly blown over by what happened next.

A voice boomed from all around, "This is Beaker blood. Very sweet. But, urgh, your friend, now that was bitter."

"So, you play with your food when you aren't hungry?" said Umov.

"No. You are wrong. What is a Beaker doing with a sword?"

"It is not what it seems. I would never hurt anyone."

"Should I believe you?"

"I apologise, but I am not permitted to say why."

"I know. You see, I was once a member of the Brotherhood too." Umov was speechless. "In my previous life I was a Beaker too. I can remember because I have not yet reincarnated."

Umov smiled, "You are still a faery. Will you spare my life?"

"I thought the answer to that was obvious by now. You will want to see the Pict you captured?"

"No, not unless Norbold the barrow-dweller is dead. You couldn't go and check for me could you? Oh, I do hope my days as his war-mask polisher and helmet-shiner are over"

"I will go and see. Wait here until I return."

"Thank you. My name is Umov EjeGod, son of the wise woman Boedil. EjeGod means Evergood in the Babel tongue."

"I am the Woodwose. That means Woodwose in every tongue."

Umov was sure that he could see a smile beneath that woody exterior.

Chapter 12: The NEW AGE

The Gridolers were waking up and, in spite of the mutterings, grumbles, and groans, they were none the worse for their ordeal. Black-Back flew onto Aniel's shoulder and screeched a little too loudly for the Gridolers tender heads.

"News from Hronesness," said Aniel.

"We heard," roared the Gridolers.

Aniel continued. "With the aid of the Picts, the Doggertae fighters, under Fecir's command, have defeated the enemy. Reports are also coming in that all the Orci trespassers who entered Sunna through the burnt Tajem were drowned."

"For me that is both sad news and a blessing," called Umov, walking towards Aniel.

"One of my captors," exclaimed Brude on sighting him. "Seize him, but do not harm him, yet."

The Woodwose floated in front of Umov. "Let him be. I will vouch for him but he must tell his own story."

"What is this?" said Brude. "Am I not master of this realm?"

"Rest easy, all will be clear soon. Will you heed my request?"

The wind picked up and it started to rain. It was probably Pan, counterbalancing Thoth's unnatural good weather earlier.

"Aye, I will old friend. But let us gather in the great hall."

The exhausted company trudged as quickly as possible into the hall, where Umov related the tale of his people to all the representatives of the free folk.

"Do you speak for the people of Orcades?" asked Aniel.

"I believe so, even if they should choose a new Jarl when I go home. All of the Orci warriors came to this battle. As such, they have broken their agreement with the Beakers. Orcades has no protection at the moment."

'The alpha time-passage has ended,' thought Volas.

"We may be able to help," said Brude. "The world has changed and, knowing that we were both right and wrong about the Orci, peaceful times may be ahead."

"What will you do as a race Brude, now that your country is divided?" asked Aniel, who was concerned that too many Picts might move towards Belevedon.

"I shall remain as the head carer of an undivided nation until I die. Thereafter, leaders of each domain shall go their own way. Any Pict currently living west of Manni shall live in southern Ru, south of the oak forest. The Taezali will no longer be nomads, but will settle as close to the Ru sea as possible. This means that our tribe will be split between the west and east of Manni. With all your blessings, the area established for the meetings of the free folk must be moved to AnTara." An emotional Brude paused to compose himself.

"And what of the Picts left east of Manni now, since the flood, and of Lutrin and Lucknow's plans?" asked Aniel anxiously.

"Lutrin and Lucknow's new tribe will reside as was planned and agreed beforehand. As for the Picts now north of Belevedon, they should move into the unoccupied northern territory of the Island, south of Orcades. They will take up guardianship of the Beakers. This is fitting, since it was the Orci warriors who made the land habitable."

"But why don't the Picts east of Manni just stay where they are?" quizzed Aniel.

"Because the Gridolers will need more land. As such, the central part of the eastern Island should be shared and open to all. Even now, different races will become dependant upon one another both for trade and survival. As long as we stay together we shall always be free."

"Brude, you have given more than you should. I am at a loss as to what we Finns can offer."

"Oh, you have much to offer, and I'm sure that you will fulfil your potential. Greater is the trust we place in you. As guardians of Belevedon you must protect us all from other people that see these Islands as a place of rich pickings. In addition, you have allies and trading partners in far off lands. For example, the tea you gave us is not from these waters is it? You will trade on our behalf."

"You are being more shrewd than you appear. We too must trust you. It has not gone unnoticed that our paths to Portowest will be surrounded on one side by men in the north and Picts in the South. Nevertheless, I am in agreement with your plan."

"Then we will leave the arrangements for those better organised than I," said Brude.

(Umov welcomed Brude's words, and people. He also decided to keep the name Orci. "The very name should keep us safe for a while yet," he laughed. Word was sent to Robin and Fecir, who also agreed with the proceedings. They were actually quite relieved to think that they would not be as isolated as they had first thought).

"Brude, we Finns will not always reside here," said Aniel.

"And neither will we Picts. Pan has told me that within six thousand years only humans will be left here."

"Did he explain?"

"It coincides with the coming of the beast's first head."

"But I thought that Thoth was dead."

"Gone," said Amergin, "but not 'dead'. You see, he designed this world and set in motion a way of being that will not change. All physical life can only exist at the expense of another life, be it plant or animal. In addition, all physical life takes more than it gives back. As a sentient being Thoth no longer makes choices that affect this world, but his spirit's original deed is unchanged and humans are easy prey to his shadow. The shadow may yet ride the beast."

The hall went quiet.

"So, all has been in vain?" Tilli said sadly.

The hall was ominously quiet. Pan, who normally tried to cheer them up was noticeably absent.

'Where are you old friend?' pleaded Brude. "Pan did make some good forecasts though," he said slowly and carefully, his words filling the silence, "within all humans will be an unconscious memory. Although they are born in human form, some of them will have the spirit of a Pict, even an Elf now that Lucknow has a soul, some will be like Gridolers and others will have the spirit of the offspring resulting from the new tribe in Athelney."

"How may one tell the difference?" asked Aniel.

"In a way similar as one does today," continued Pan with much merriment. "There's no disguising Gridolers' noses are there." Aniel didn't react; his gaze remaining on Brude.

"Pan!" exclaimed a delighted Lutrin, "you have this knack of turning up when someone is thinking about you."

"Wherever two or more are gathered in my name, there I am in the midst of them," he teased, "but let me continue with what I have seen. Seriously, these humans will have an aura about them. Those astute enough to see it, will see pointed ears on some people. Others, because they are really Gridolers inside, get mistaken for being grumpy, and yet the most grumpy people I met actually had a heart of gold."

"Not surprising," said Malceni, "given their love for it."

"But changing the subject back to what Amergin said about all life 'taking' and not 'giving'. There is an exception to the rule," said Lutrin.

"I know this one as well," said Malceni.

"Explain then," urged Lutrin.

"It was Amergin, when he was being Thoth that gave us a clue. Or was it Thoth when he was in Amergin".

"Never mind Malceni!" spluttered Amergin.

"Well it's a tree you see," continued Malceni.

"But a tree 'takes' water and sunlight," said Brude trying to catch him out, but not dismissing the importance of trees.

"A tree," said Lutrin, "may take water, but it will give it back when it dies. Indeed, even the minerals it takes from the soil are given back in death. Meanwhile, it bestows more than it takes. Apart from its beauty, it cleans the air and provides food and homes for many creatures."

"And the sunlight it absorbs?" asked Malceni.

"It is a mystery, but for some reason I think that the sun and the moon are, well .. actually they are trees. Or trees are actually the sun and moon. The light from both gives light to each other. I can't explain it further, sorry."

"I think I can Lu," said Malceni, "remember that little verse you told me?"

"No," Lutrin began to say; but Malceni had already started,

"'From sun to leaf,
And root below ground,
The sacred fire
There can be found.

And from Moon to leaf,
And root below ground.
Your inner-earth therein is fed,
A light to raise Finn from the dead'."

Not one for songs as a rule, Malceni had been feeling so good because he had started one; that he exclaimed the last line quite loudly and raised his arms in the air.

Pan sniggered, but everyone else in the hall fell silent.

"Oh Mal," groaned Brude.

"Dear me," said Lutrin.

"Oops," said Tilli in Malceni fashion.

"What? What's the problem?" asked a dejected Malceni.

"There are certain things," retorted an angry Aniel, "that neither race should share with another."

"The profanity of the vain," muttered Malceni.

Pan was laughing so much now that he had to leave the hall.

"With the Gridolers it is their language," continued an exasperated Aniel. "The Finnic are not permitted to share everything either. However, what I can say is this. There is more truth in what Lutrin told you than many could realise, or even believe, if I told them. That knowledge came from within him, and yet it is only known to the Finni of old."

"No Finn from amongst the Finni or the Finnic has told me this," said Lutrin.

"I know, because Finns can not use the words in the same way. But you are a mystery," he said frowning.

"I am tired after all the battles Aniel," said Lutrin smiling, "please do not go there my friend." A shadow passed before Aniel. "I must get some sleep. But for the record, I know you meant no ill. I forgive you. I always will. And I hope you forgive Malceni, for at times he knows not what he does. Now, goodnight."

Lutrin bowed to everyone and left for his tree house. Most of those gathered there also decided it was time to retire - including the Gridolers - who were more than a little tipsy.

Malceni had no intention of apologising, even though one had not been asked of him, and left the hall mumbling, "Finnic Finni Finns. Blah. Give me an ordinary straight forward Elf any day." 'Which reminds me,' he thought, 'I will not wait a moment more. I have put this off too long.' He headed towards Titch's tree. Malceni had a question for her, and he hoped the answer would be 'yes'.'

Aniel didn't notice them saying goodnight, for he was too engrossed with Lutrin's final words. He had heard those words before, years earlier, one night in Athelney after the gathering. He heard those words again, echoing in his mind, 'Please. Do not go there my friend. Do not delve too far .... I needed a rest. Helping him is helping me. Helping me, helps you .... remember 'I am.'

"He is right," muttered Aniel to himself, "best to let sleeping dogs rest."

*

The following morning, Titch turned up with all her belongings at the tree hut above Malceni's tree. The problem was that Malceni had been using the hut, because he preferred it to being downstairs.

Titch walked in to the stench of Pan's leaf and unwashed ale jugs. She was not pleased.

"What a dung hole," she said.

"I didn't think you'd say 'yes' no soon," said a sleepy Malceni.

"I don't think I will now."

"Sorry."

"Get it sorwted and move downstairws, orw I weally will be angwy," she replied, storming off to see Lucknow.

He noticed that she had left her belongings in the doorway. "I'll take that as a 'yes' then," he said smiling.

Lutrin helped Malceni get the hut all spick-and-span. He was about to remove all the luxuries that Malceni had acquired on his travels down to the tree house. "No," said Malceni, "leave them Lu. Like a queen to me shall she be." They both left to get some breakfast. Lucknow and Titch, who had been waiting for them to leave, went over to the tree. "I am happy for you," said Lucknow.

Titch couldn't believe the transformation. 'Maybe he doesn't need too much twaining afterwall,' thought Titch. She had a little tear in her eye. Malceni was famed for his comforts, but he had left them all for her. A bunch of flowers had been placed on the table, next to a note that read, *'For my little Titch, 'sorry', Lots of love, Mal x.'* "Give me a hand Lu," she asked, "to get some of these things downstairws."

When Lutrin and Malceni returned, Lucknow and Titch were waiting with a pot of tea. "She makes the best cup in Sunna," said Malceni, in ear shot of Titch.

*

The end of the numerous migrations that year had ended, and the Islands were a far better place for it. Now it was time for a great celebration around the Meare. A bonding was about to take place and all of the company would once again be assembled. The faeries who had not stayed in Bryhery Gap followed Lutrin to his new home, where, for the first time, they met the divas; the plant and flower faeries who helped all vegetation to grow.

As soon as Brude arrived, Lutrin called him to one side. Before his new life was to begin in earnest, he wanted to know the answer to the unanswered question.

'Father, what happened to the Bryhery Gap?'

"It has changed Lutrin, like everything else. But it is the right thing," Brude tried to put forward a brave face, because he didn't want to spoil his son's bonding night.

"Where has it gone to?"

"To many places. A little bit of it is everywhere. Some is here, around Meare. But the places are often too small for people to see anymore. It will function in the same way, as an in-between home. But it may as well have gone from this world altogether. Pan tells me there is another Gap growing, called Avalon, but he refuses to tell me more. Ah, even change that is right can often feel sad. Your mother grieves for the past. She is here by the way. Let us go and see her."

"You both miss the Gap don't you?" asked Lutrin.

"Yes, my poika, we do," said Volas.

"We will speak of this later," he said, "when I give you my present. It is a tradition I am going to start. If it is your birthday, instead of getting presents from your friends you should give them a present instead."

"But this is a bonding, not a birthday party."

"Yes, but I might not always get a chance to share my ideas with you. Besides, it is a birthday of sorts. It is the birth of a new town."

"You've decided on a name then?" said Brude happily.

"I hadn't given it much thought, too much to do you see.

So, I thought I would stick with an idea that Pan gave me. It will be called Picton."

"A solid name," said Brude, "with good foundations."

"Perhaps. But I foresee the name being lost. In time, things are forgotten that ought not to be. When did you last celebrate our Firbolgian roots?"

"I see your point," said Brude, but his thoughts were elsewhere.

"There is an answer to your thoughts on where the Finns go," said Lutrin. "The ships from Portowest are a medium for light travel; a sort of Finnic Bryhery Gap for Finns still living; similar to the bridges I can make. This explains how Panara was saved. You see, a part of Lucknow went the way it should have, but it left a gap, no pun intended. Nature abhors a vacuum. There was Panara, who has a soul but no transitionary place to go. She merged with Lucknow's body in the hope of entering the Bryhery Gap. Then, the unexpected happens, Aniel revives her. As to the Finns. They head north-west, past the Mithras cave on Innis Muidr, and on towards a tiny island called Rockall. En-route they merge with the light of the rising Sun and the ship gradually rises into the air. Very tiny movements, edding upwards. And then, just before sunset, as the light merges with the moonlight, they reach a dimension that only a Finnic spirit can enter."

"None other can enter?" enquired Volas, anxious to ensure that he had heard correctly.

"None. Furthermore, you must have Finnic blood in you, albeit only a tiny amount is needed, from some distant relation perhaps."

"How did you discover this out?" Brude interjected.

"I visited the place. Just to have a peek."

"You didn't?" exclaimed a shocked Volas. "But how did you enter?"

"I truly do not know. They weren't very pleased," he said laughing. He imitated what he had heard, "'Your time is not yet' boomed a voice from the sky. This is all I remember, for somehow something did not want me to remember; that it was the most wondrous place I have ever experienced."

Aniel had been listening in astonishment. "In truth, it makes you sorrowful at times, doesn't it?"

"Ha," said Lutrin smiling, "still snooping eh?" But then the smile dropped and that same far away expression, so often observed as a child when he was about to 'have one of his episodes', overtook his face. His tura began to project,

'Ah, to breath its air and see the hills,

In the blessed realm of true Karelia;

To walk in the fair forests of the Tallinium,

And to drink the waters of the white spring.'

"Sorrowful," said Lutrin, "yes ... because I am no longer there. Now I know why you sometimes look a little grim."

Although he couldn't hold back his tears, it was now Aniel's turn to smile. "That was the most precious personal gift I have received since the dawn of the Alpha-Age. No words could express my gratitude. You Pict-tura'd the place of my birth Lutrin. I could even smell ... ." He could hardly speak, as the memory burden of a thousand years pressed hard upon his shoulders. " ... the light-blue grass and the Tallin tree blossom."

Aniel's face was radiant, as he grinned from ear to ear. "It is my hope to return there one day, " he said, "and, perhaps yourself. But you should not really speak openly of these things."

"Why not?"

"If all life's mysteries are explained then where is the fun and learning from self-discovery."

"There are always mysteries in the world," replied Brude. "Besides, Volas and I are getting a little old for much more self-discovery."

"In this lifetime perhaps," commented Aniel.

Lutrin heard someone calling him. "Let us join the crowd," he said. As he moved, he pulled Aniel to one side. "I do not always speak of such things but I have a feeling that my mother and father will be leaving us soon. If they accept my gift that is. If so, they may never incarnate again. You see, I intend to send them on a one-way journey. I can't go with them because I fear getting trapped, but they will want to go."

"What is this gift?"

"I will open a bridge for them. A bridge to a tiny world. To the Bryhery Gap they will go and stay for as long as they like."   *

It looked like the whole countryside was covered in tents. Thousands had turned out for the biggest single celebration the Island had ever seen. For tonight there was more than one bonding, there were hundreds of them. It was eight o'clock in the evening, on Sunday the nineteenth of November, and this night would always be remembered as a night for feasting. Lutrin had chosen this night specifically to coincide with the coming of that year's Urinox, the day the dead visited the living. In Picton, the actual date changed each year, because they still lived according to the movements of the moon and not the sun, which was how humans lived.

Although the Finns, Elfin and Gridolers did not relish this moment, their human friends understood the significance of this Pictish occasion. Lutrin had also wanted a day later on in the year, to give them all a chance of finishing their houses. The ceremony would take place at the foot of Meare Tor, close to the river Caelis. Each couple began by walking around the Tor in a spiral. Along the way, the Urs greeted them with words of advice. UrBred came alongside Lutrin.

"Grandfather."

"My dear Lu. Only a short time as usual. Who needs me more, you or my son?"

"I think you should tell Brude your plans. It will make my suggestion to him later all the easier to accept."

"A wise decision. Goodbye then, for the last time. My best wishes and good luck to you both."

"Thank you," said Lucknow. UrBred disappeared, much to her delight even though she didn't show it.

"Lucknow," said Lutrin.

"Yes," she replied.

He looked deep into her eyes and recognised the gaze she gave him, "I know we haven't talked about it, but you know that you have Panara's eyes?"

"Of course, I see them in the mirror everyday, don't I?"

Lucknow found it much easier to talk about certain things than Lutrin did. "The eyes are the mirror of the soul. But my spirit is still that of Lucknow. It is you that seems to have issues about this, not I."

"Your hair smells lovely tonight," he said teasingly.

"Very funny," she said. "Enough of this. Let's go and enjoy tonight's entertainment."

Many people started running over to where the Gridolers would perform. The idea that such tough and rough looking people would be singing and dancing, was a sight not to be missed. Deedle had promised them a song that encompassed all musical genres; a fitting scenario for a spirit whose name meant 'All'.

With what sounded like a didgeridoo, Deedle blew down his 'Dord iseal' pipe, and Pliny trumpeted on the 'Dord ard' horn. Two Picts drummed up the beat with their giant 'Bodhrans', and Garaldina joined them with her lyre.

Tilli stepped forward to sing:

'Pan and the Ice-age Rock'

Oh Pan, what a mystery,

Good and kind, full of dread can be,

Saw the ice, going on too long,

Stamped his feet, and it was gone

Oh Pan, Oh Pan, Oh Pan.

Whilst chanting the 'Oh Pan' chorus, the Gridolers stamped their feet and turned in a circle; on one foot only. The ground shook every time. After the end of each 'Oh Pan'; Garaldina skimmed the strings of her lyre and Deedle blew an 'E flat' tone deeply on the 'Adharc' horn.

The cold came, from the northern way,

For what felt like, forever and a day,

Pan saw it going on to long,

Stamped his feet and it was gone,

Oh Pan, Oh Pan, Oh Pan.

Oh Pan ended Island misery,

Made it warm, as the sun can be,

Give him thanks, but not your praise,

A head on the beast, just ain't his game.

Oh Pan, Oh Pan, Oh Pan, Oh Pan, Oh Pan.

Joining them, Pan played his Pipes during the verses. As he did so, he danced and strutted in and out of the Gridolers. The Gridolers didn't seem to notice him, but they became more entranced in their routine with each strut. The energy of all the players seemed to envelope everyone watching in to the group. They had become participants and not just observers. By this point, nearly all those present were copying the Gridolers chant and movements. All the tables and chairs started bouncing up and down. Many more Picts also took up the beat with their drums each time that Tilli sang 'Oh Pan'. Arms were being waved and heads started rocking to the beat.

Give him thanks, but not your praise,

A god of the Ark*, just ain't his game.

Oh Pan, Oh Pan, Oh Pan.

Warning give, and warnings gave,

If you ignore the truth, Pan will stamp again.

On You, and You, and You.

* Theological considerations were given to this idea until the early 20th century.

The Gridolers kept pointing at people as they stamped around. This started off clapping to the beat during both the verse and chorus. Those not dancing or clapping, banged their mugs on the table and stamped their feet. The Finnic sang a single angelic like crescendo to each 'Oh Pan', accompanied by the 'Crothall' bells of Ru.

He'll bring you down, if you don't behave,
Rearrange your face, put you in the grave.
So whatever you do, don't ignore the wave.
Oh Pan, Oh Pan, Oh Pan.

Give him thanks, but not your praise,
The occult, just ain't his game.
Give him thanks, but not your praise,
The occult, just ain't his game.
 Oh Pan, Oh Pan, Oh Pan, Oh Pan, Oh Pan.

Cheers erupted, with shouts for an encore, but the Gridolers had only practiced one song, so they bowed low and joined the rest of the gathering.

Meanwhile, UrBred was visiting Brude. "My son. How goes the day?"

"Very well Father. I saw you visiting Lu."

UrBred nodded. "This is the last time you will see me. It is time for me to continue my path and become faery."

"I have a final question for you Father," said Brude. "Did you find my stewardship acceptable? Did I honour our forefathers?"

"It seems that, regardless of age, a son always desires approval from his father. Yes Brude, you guided your people well through a crisis not of your making and you reared a great poika. Go back to the Bryhery Gap and rest."

"What do you mean?"

"Oh, sorry. I shouldn't have said that."

"Out with it. Tradition demands nothing less."

UrBred went on to tell Brude and Volas what Lutrin was planning. Both looked at the other and nodded in unison. They would go the Gap.

*

Brude, Aniel and Pan stood side by side with Aniel sandwiched between them. "Today", he said, "a new age begins. An intimate alliance of Elf and Pict." Aniel felt that Brude was standing too close and stepped back a little.

"Yes," agreed Brude. "An alliance built out of both necessity and love."

'And on genetics,' thought Pan. He saw many Picts frowning, 'Sorry, I shouldn't have thought that'.

"In maintaining a balance," he said, " I can not say further than this. To put it simply, the fruit of this union will go unnoticed. And yet, at the right moment, this fruit could well shape the future of the world. Long life and happiness to all your simple fruit."

Pan's grin was, as usual, disarming.

"I could swing for him. What does he mean simple fruit," said Malceni poking Lutrin on the shoulder from behind.

"Not now eh Mal,"

Umov's grey-haired old mother, Boedil, stepped forward. She was covered in scars.

"May the peace of Mithras be with you always," she said.

The crowd responded with, "And also with you."

"All you need do," she continued, "in order to ratify your bonding, is to jump over the boundary stone together and shout 'I love you.' Then you must retire to your homes and, an hour later, assemble in the festival tent. Let the bondings begin."

After waiting for silence, Lutrin and Lucknow jumped. "I love you," they both shouted. Malceni and Titch went next. Titch was not her real name. Being one of the smallest Elfin and having a lisp, Malceni used to tease her a lot. Eventually, the name 'Titch' stuck and the teasing turned to love. A huge cheer, and shouts of celebration came from the crowd. After a while, all that could be heard was a constant "I love you" which then became a mantra. Thousands of people started chanting, 'love' over and over again. The energy from this constant tone began to vibrate along the ground. The vibration intensified. "Love, love." The trees began to shiver. It was like the feeling a person gets when they first wake up the morning and have a stretch. "Love, love." The tips of the grasses and the leaves began to glow.

'Mmm,' thought Pan, 'They have almost hit the right tone, nearly there.'

The crowd were as one.

The people who had bonded had returned to their houses, but the crowd continued, "love, love."

The air began to buzz and whistle. "Love, love, love."

The sky stopped and the air began to light up. The chanting became louder. The crowd felt as if the earth was spinning faster and faster until it became so fast that time stood still. And then, in unison, they all stopped.

From a tiny island in the middle of Meare came a whooshing sound. The water flattened, and lit up like moonlight on glass. And then they saw them. Faeries. Faeries came pouring in from the island.

"Yes!" exclaimed Pan, stamping his feet. "They did it! They did it!" He began to hum, 'Oh Pan.'

"The Bryhery Gap of Middle-Meare," said Volas. "Somehow, I don't think we will be going far after all."

"It is back," cried Brude. "My Bryhery Gap is back."

"It's quite small though, isn't it?" said Pan. "Just enough work for two I would say."

It was a very small Gap, but big enough for people to see it, for a little while each day as it circumnavigated the Meare.

"Thank you my dear old love," said Volas. Brude was not offended.

"It was the love that did it. Yes, I prepared the way for it, but love triumphed, not magic."

"The whole world changed tonight Pan. Only a little speck, but it did change".

"I told you Brude," said Pan, rather pleased with himself, "I am a conduit. Do you know, for a moment, I thought Thoth was helping. The Thoth who's returned to his source, not his shadow that lies heavily upon you. Perhaps he is trying to change."

"Do not go there," said Volas, "you always said to me when I was young, 'Volas. I am.'" She sang, "Speculation just ain't your game."

"You are right of course," replied Pan. "Why didn't I think of that earlier. Anyway, must dash. Give my regards to Lutrin and Panara. Oh." He paused for a moment.

'Poor Pan,' thought Volas.

"Sorry, I meant Lucknow," he continued.

"I feel sorry for humans," said Volas to Brude, "they don't see what we see or feel how we feel."

"Most of them anyway. But someone, one day, will tell the world the truth about us. And then my love, on that day, his spark will ignite a never-ending flame."

Chapter 13: **TIBBOHA of PICTON**

At 8.30am on the 21st August in the year 1, by Picton reckoning (*they didn't want to start with a Zero*), a cry was heard from the first breath of a Picton baby. Lutrin had dug another room in the hillside, but it wasn't really needed as he had already dug out more than enough rooms. One of them led to the opening of a huge chasm filled with Blue-John.

The Blue-John had made Picton a wealthy town because Lutrin shared the precious stone with his people. Tilli had helped to train some of the Picton folk to work with the stone, enabling them to make beautiful crafts from the Blue-John. Not being miners, the Finns only ever saw Blue-John from the surface, which is why they called it Vasa Murrhina. Vasa had a purple band, a white band and a band of both. Blue-John from the mine was mainly purple, with a dash of yellow. The seam most prized by Gridolers was the very rare section that contained elements of all three colours.

Tilli had remained for a while in the Dwelfish mountains because he had discovered gold at the end of the seam originally provided by the Finns. He found one small rock, shaped like the end of a tree root, containing the rare tri-colour Blue-John and some gold. Using all of his skill, he fashioned a pair of earrings from it. 'So beautiful are they that even Thoth could not gaze for long upon them, lest it turn his heart to good,' thought Tilli. When he next saw Lutrin, he handed the earrings to him and said that they should be given to the first female born to either Malceni or himself.

Lutrin entered Lucknow's room.

"What is it?" he asked.

"'It,' is a 'he'," she replied.

"Good. I mean, a 'she' would have been just as welcome, but good." This was one hole that he couldn't dig his way out of very well. "And his name?"

"I have seen the name mirrored in your tura many times, ever since you built the house that you gave to Taesus."

'Tibboha?' thought Lutrin.

"Yes. His name is Tibboha."

"Let me see him my love."

"Wonderful, simply wonderful," he said, quietly slipping the earrings back into his pocket.

*

The new child, the first of the Tibbohan race, was born with a thick mat of blonde hair. Not until his 'tweens' did his hair turn brown. Although he had dark brown eyes, they shone like the Moon and at times it was like looking into a scrying mirror. He was also born with wide hairy feet. Most striking of all was the pointed ears, and the tiny little horns beneath his hair.

"Useful for keeping one's hat on," Tibboha would say in later life. Lutrin was the only Pict with pointed ears, so thankfully, like Lucknow and Lutrin, the rest of the tribes babies had pointed ears. The ear-point was not as pronounced as the Finns or Elfin, but was proportionate to their overall build. Only the off-spring of Tibboha would ever have those tiny bumps; a remnant of the horns.

None of the Tibbohans ever grew more than three feet three inches. As the years would pass, it would be apparent that the children would have neither the Picts' ability to tura nor be able to communicate telepathically.

Meanwhile, Pan called in from time to time and told the children stories about wizards and the dragon of Mam Tor. 'He had made them all up of course,' thought Lutrin, 'or Tilli would have mentioned it.' Wizards did not come off very well in Pan's stories. 'Nature's manipulators' he often called them. This probably explained why three years later, when Amergin finally paid Picton a visit, all of the children in Picton had hid from him. Malceni and Titch were also having tea at the time with Lutrin and Lucknow. Titch had recently given birth to Margaret on the 24th October.

"Margaret," said Amergin, "how did you decide on that?"

"Fwom Taesus actually," said Titch, "apawently its all the wage in Wu."

"Trouble with her warz," whispered Lutrin in Amergin's ear.

"Ah, yes I did hear so little Titch."

"Aw you twying to be funny Amewin?" said Titch, rather annoyed.

"No dear," said Malceni. "It's a term of endearment. Amergin called us all little when we were younger." She nodded an acceptance of his explanation.

"How are the children developing?" enquired Amergin.

"Pan says they are perfectly healthy and normal. As for ancient abilities, they have few," said Lucknow.

"Like little humans you mean?"

"Not exactly," said Lutrin. They have my ability to merge with their background. Thereafter, it is their normal senses that have been heightened; far stronger than humans. They also have an empathic link to all nature and living things. Stronger than the Finnic. Pan said that they will one day show us how to improve our brew making, and that they will be able to grow almost anything in any terrain in any weather condition. They are very attuned to the faery Devas."

"Mithras must be proud of them," said Amergin, "it means they have a love for life far greater than any previous race."

"Who is this Mithwas anyway?" said Titch, "Oh please excuse me, Mawgwets cwying." Malceni breathed a sigh of relief when she went into one of the spare bedrooms.

Tears were rolling down Lutrin's face. "Don't start Lu, she could be back any second."

"I know," he said, still laughing, "I can't help it. I twuly am sowwy."

"I came to say goodbye", said Amergin, "I've decided to go home".

"So you will miss the opening night of my Pub!" said Malceni, "It is called 'The Bracken Bryher', but I suppose people will shorten it to B&B."

"When you've seen one, you've seen them all."

"You are tired of life then!"

"I did read your 'drinks list' sign outside."

"The paint is still drying."

"Very inventive," continued Amergin, "but where you got the idea for 'The Wizard's Finger' ale from is not quite clear."

"From you of course."

"Yes, but you refer to it as 'a sharp gaseous brew'."

"My favourite is his 'Firbolg Winter Brew'," said Lutrin, "'a strong dark ale'."

"Don't forget the Finnic non-alcoholic wine," said Lucknow, "that was my idea."

"We even have a special guest drink," Malceni reminded them, "it is a very strong spirit, distilled from Pictish heather ale by the Gridolers. Would you like to try some?"

"That would be most welcome, far more so than the 'The Wizard's Finger,'" he frowned, continuing, "which sounds quite vulgar."

"I have some GS with Valerian root tea, just before bed," said Lutrin, "it helps me get to sleep."

Malceni poured Amergin an unusually large glass of GS: 'Gridolers Spirit'. "A world without wizards," said Malceni, "I can't say I'll be sorry. Nothing personal."

Not realising its potency, Amergin drank the spirit as quickly as he might an ale. "Oh there will be wizards," smiled Amergin, as the alcohol began entering his blood stream, "Mithras, in physical form, is not too far away, and my two other brothers will be coming as well."

"That is all we need," said Pan, popping his head around the door, "three of you at the same time ... why are you smiling so much?"

Amergin frowned, "I don't recall your name being mentioned."

This time Pan became serious. "What are your brothers like?"

Amergin took another sip and thought for a moment. "Well Mithras is a bit like me, you know, modest!"

'Please spare us!' thought Pan.

Lutrin laughed. "I heard that Pan," said Amergin. "As for the others, one is quite serious. Thinks he does the right thing all the time. Makes many mistakes though, so Mithras has put him in charge, for now, to help with his self-development."

"And the third?" asked Malceni.

"A bit of a loner really. Doesn't like getting involved."

"An unusual trait for a wizard," said Pan, "perhaps I might get on with him."

"That is all I can tell you about their physical form," finished Amergin.

"Do you mean that their actual nature can change?" questioned Pan.

"Oh yes," replied Amergin, "for good or ill."

"Whose idea was it to send all three brothers?"

"It was Thoth's actually. He thought it might make the world of difference."

"And while Mithras is away ... Let me guess, you will watch over Thoth?"

"Don't worry. There will be more than just myself there. He will do no harm."

"It seems he has already done enough," growled Pan, "you're a fool Amergin." He turned to Lutrin. "Warn all your children Lutrin, never meddle in a wizard's business, unless, until ... oh never mind. I'll see you another time." Pan bowed to all, but to Amergin he requested a word outside.

Outside the house, Pan focused his gaze on Amergin, quizzing, "When you have gone, where and when will the wizards arrive?"

"In Portowest on Mithras' birthday," said Amergin, "the 25th December, just after I leave."

"Please grant me a favour."

"If I can."

Pan handed him a little box. "Aniel gave me this. He said I would know who it should go to."

"I'm listening."

"Give this to the harbour master and ask him to 'give it to the wisest wizard who arrives'. It contains a fragment of the AnTara tree of light."

"I will make it so, for I understand something of Aniel's hope. The Finns believe that if the power of their two ancient trees was brought together then their light would dissolve the shadow of Thoth. The second fragment is yet to be found."

"Thank you. Aniel puts more trust in wizards than I am able to," Pan said sadly.

"And yet," said Amergin, "he sees you as the one who can help bring balance to this affair."

"How so?"

"You could not bring yourself to directly choose a particular wizard, and yet a wizard is still your medium. Within that, you have asked the harbour master to choose. Aniel could not bring himself to hand over the fragment to a human, and yet he knows that the prophecy says that without humans the shadow will remain."

"Please tell the others we did not part on bad terms."

"I will," said Amergin, going back inside and draining his cup of the last of his drink.

Whilst Amergin was holding this conversation, Malceni and Lutrin were holding one of their own.

"I've only just realised," said Malceni, "that I never saw a Gridoler actually talking to Pan. In fact, even the Finns regarded him more as a shadow. The Elfin heard him. But only Picts and humans truly saw and heard him in the same way."

"But what about Amergin?" asked Lutrin.

"Amergin saw him like us, but only when a Pict was in the vicinity."

"Come to think of it Malceni, the only human we know that saw him that way was Taesus."

"You are right and, given his link to us, we shouldn't be too surprised."

"I may be able to explain," said Lucknow. "The Gridolers only 'saw' Pan in stone and water beneath the mountain.

Did you notice when they sang their song about him, that they didn't acknowledge him dancing around them; but that they heard him. And it was like the tinkling of water to them; they knew he was with them. They also accepted the fact that Picts could see and talk with him, which is why they never interrupted you. We Elfin were not brought up to see him that way, but we were born with the ability to do so, so he became much clearer after we met you. As for Finns, they too see him differently. In fact, they believe that they see him better than you do."

Just as she had finished speaking, Lutrin was sure that she had turned her nose upwards.

"Typical Aniel arrogance," said Malceni through gritted teeth, "jealousy more like. I didn't once see them talk to Pan."

Lucknow glared at him.

"I think it is obvious that the Tibbohans see Pan more easily," said Lutrin, turning away.

When Amergin returned, Lutrin asked him why Pan held wizards in low esteem.

"You should ask him yourself," said Amergin rather abruptly. His head was spinning.

"I am asking you though."

Amergin took a deep breath. "He thinks we are manip .... hic ... manipulative. But if we are then it is in a good way. Take today for example," he said, belching out breath that would have shamed a dog, "I'm leaving, but I couldn't help but gather some information for Mithras, about your new tribe. We like to see where all the bits of the puzzle fit in."

"You mean, how you can use people?"

"It is not like that," he replied wagging his head and finger.

Caught unawares, Amergin had no time to react. Lutrin had used his tura, and Malceni was using his tura to increase Lutrin's strength, to eradicate all memory of the tribes children from Amergin's mind. Amergin blinked. "Where was I. Yes. I didn't see any children when I arrived."

"Such is life," said Lutrin.

"Never mind. Some things are not meant to be," Amergin responded, with his head still nodding.

"Aye, that's true. Well it was nice to see you before you left for good."

"What about the Roc?" asked Malceni.

"Take this Mal. It was meant for Picton's first born but you keep it. It is a whistle, to call the Roc. After dropping me off in Portowest, she's off to better hunting grounds. I hope she will be okay, she's been a bit moody lately."

Amergin tapped his nose to indicate that he was keeping a secret. But when they said nothing to him, he seemed to forget what it was he was going to say. "Anyway, goodbye."

Amergin, still quite dazed, stood up, and walked outside.

They never saw him again.

"We did right Lu," said Malceni, "hopefully, the tall folk will leave us alone from now on."

"Perhaps. For a while at least. Perhaps. Tibbs' whistle please". Reluctantly, he handed Lutrin the Roc's whistle.

"I do have something for Margaret though, well it's from Tilli actually," continued Lutrin, who proceeded to tell him about the earrings.

"I actually beat you to something then," said Malceni. "Wow, these must be worth a fortune."

"Yes. Over thousands of years, minerals from trees form part of the stone. Brude once told me that a violent shock can fracture the unique crystalline structure, resulting in the colour disappearing. That could be why Blue-John is desired so much. Moonlight itself has stopped to rest in a stone. Do you remember that night we escaped from Manni and Tarquin called upon the light of Gilwain's hidden star?"

"I forgot to ask him about that," replied Malceni.

"Tarquin had some Blue-John. Apparently, you can't see Gilwain's star but it is there shining all the time. The moonlight in Tarquin's stone can reflect the hidden starlight."

"So, in practical terms, it is a perfect example of how Moonlight lights up anything precious that is hidden," said Malceni. "You said Tarquin had some of the stone."

Smiling, Lutrin pulled a stone from his pocket and showed it to Malceni. "He said he could always get another one. He wanted me to have it because I was the first person he had seen, not of his kind, who had activated it."

After sharing a pipe and a cup of tea, Lutrin asked Malceni if he ever got to the bottom of the unpleasant vision he had had in the mirror. Malceni nodded and told him that it was an alternative time-line. In it, Malceni had never been kept in the Gap when he was younger and, as such, kept having problems in the outside world.

"Let's have a look now," said Lutrin.

"No need, I wrote it down. It helped somehow. However, as soon as you have read it I must burn it."

"I understand."

Malceni handed Lutrin the story.

After reading what was written, Lutrin passed it to Malceni, who immediately put a flame to it. The imparting of this knowledge was as if a thunderbolt had passed between them, and the two sat in silence, absorbing the implications. Lutrin eventually broke the spell with the words, "That was a horrible nightmare to live with for so long. I wish I could have helped."

"When the sun still affected me, you often took images from me, which eased the pain."

"Was the Orci witch one of them?" asked Lutrin.

"You remembered. Yes, that was a scary one all right."

"Don't you think that she looked like Boedil?"

"Yes," said Malceni, "I think it was her."

"So she got away then. Good for her."

"In the other time-line, can you remember what happened to you beforehand?"

"Only that I received a blow which scraped down the entire three inch groove-hollow in the back of my skull."

Lutrin was horrified. "They knew exactly the precise spot to damage a tura. No Pict would share our secret place with another race." Lutrin paused. "I don't suppose you saw who ... .. ?"

"No," he replied. "And I'd rather not think about it."

"I understand."

Malceni paused for a moment, "Lu, you were always there for me."

"As you were for me my friend, as you were for me."

THE END

APPENDICES

APPENDIX 1

The 'MISSING' stories

A few 'stories' were omitted because it was apparent that they were only suitable once the reader became 'familiar' with the characters. In chronological order, I respectfully include them here, with notes in '*italic*' explaining their context.

'The Marche people' (Part 1):   *In chapter 5, whilst travelling to the meeting in Athelney, Uriel was going to point out a group of people to Lutrin.*

Eventually, the land became rather flat, except for a range of hills dotted around the landscape. They could not walk a direct route because vast areas were prone to flooding. Lutrin was surprised to see a small group of people living in houses on stilts. The Finns made no effort to greet them and they made none either.

"They don't see us," said Uriel, "they were the first inhabitants of this land and we suspect that they are actually retreating into a different world." As he spoke, a mist descended around the travelers. It was not a damp or cold mist; it felt more like a covering. "By the time the mist clears, most of us here will even forget that we saw them.   Aniel is able to remind other Finns of their presence." He paused and looked at Lutrin. "I wonder if you can also do so?"

Stretching some nine miles and named 'The Marches', this area marked the end of the Gridolers boundary. The mist quickly cleared as they passed into the Finnic dominated part of Belevedon. The landscape became more gentle, with rolling hills and fields.

"I do remember those people," said Lutrin.

"So do I," added Malceni proudly, who had been listening to Uriel and Lutrin earlier.

"Remember who?" questioned Uriel knowingly.

"You know," said Malceni, "those ... ones on stilts ... them. Oh I've forgotten what I was talking about now."

"The natives," said Lutrin.

"I know. For I too can recall," smiled Uriel.

'The Marche people' (Part 2): *Later on, in chapter 6, Pan took Lutrin to see the Marche people.*

"I think it's time that you met the people of the Marches," said Pan. "You saw them once before I believe. Do you remember?"

"Yes. But after the mist had cleared only a few of us could remember."

"They are nice people aren't they?"

"I don't know," said Lutrin, "I only saw them at a distance."

"You did more than that," laughed Pan, "it seems that the Finns can't even remember the Marches' hospitality. The mist does more than just hide them. Come."

A mist descended around them. Once again, it was not a cold or damp mist, it was more like a covering. A covering to hide something. They could hear voices in the mist, and the murmur of people who were enjoying going about their daily chores. There was a splash, a dog barking and the laughter of children. As the people came into view, so too did Pan and Lutrin. Some of them, but not all, ran in 'panic'; a word often associated with a fear of Pan.

The children didn't run, for they had nothing to fear from him. They were standing on a very well constructed wooden track, that was as wide as the Finnic road. In fact, it was in exactly the same place as where the Finnic road should be!

"So we are in an echo of the past. An image of those who were once here," said Lutrin.

"That is how the Finns see it. But I have 'amended' the recollections somewhat, of those that remember anything."

"I would ask, 'what are you up to?' But I'll let you play your little game."

Pan looked at Lutrin with as displeased a look that he had ever given him. "This is not a game. It is part of what I must do, always, to keep things from getting in a mess." He indicated to Lutrin to see if one of the people wanted a slice of his bread. As Lutrin stepped forward, they looked horrified and grabbed food for him instead.

"Is this because of their laws of hospitality?" asked Lutrin.

"Not at all. They have fear of your bread."

"Pardon."

"When they see you, they believe that they are channeling your energy. They think that you are dead, and to eat the food of a dead person would make them dead too. Or, that they may join you in a sort of limbo in your world."

"How peculiar," said Lutrin.

"Of course they wouldn't die if they ate your food. But they could enter your world, not in limbo though. So, in one sense, it is not as peculiar as you think."

"So they can move forward into our time?"

"Move into our time, yes, but not forward." He stopped, to allow Lutrin to pause for thought.

"But that would mean that it is they who are from the future, and not me."

"Exactly," replied Pan, "and that is why I have to ... ."

" 'Amend' recollections," interrupted Lutrin.

"Yes. These Marche people keep looking out for people like you, to learn more about their ancestral customs. The problem is that they see no harm in telling you things about what it is like in their time, because they think you are dead."

"But how do they latch on to us?"

"It is because of your future involvement in Meare. Your energy and those of your kind are creating a vibration in the earth. It will become like a magnet for all those seeking."

"Seeking what?" asked Lutrin

"Themselves," smiled Pan.

"And will they find themselves?"

"Oh yes, but only a few. Most of them settle for less," replied Pan

"In what way?"

"They settle for someone else. Someone who thinks that they have found themselves and then tells others that they have as well. They are called Gurus."

"But where is the link? We are not near Athelney."

"Go and ask them who they are."

Lutrin spoke to them, but he could understand nothing without using his tura. "I thought you said that you were concerned about dialogue," said Lutrin.

"Even without speech, you see many things and so do the Finns. In fact we can pick up more information than the Avalonians can."

"Yes," said Lutrin, "I do not recognise the name; but that would seem an appropriate term for them. Again, what of the link."

"Oh yes, sorry. Well, the story of the Avalonians is this. They will live a few miles south-west of Ganjara, not far from the Helsby Tor that overlooks the Tavae estuary of the Nabarus river. Just off the coast is a little island, the Isle of Avalon they will call it. This Isle will come and go with the mists. I will not tell you more about that part until much later in this story. One day, people will look to Avalon for guidance; in the same way that they are looking for you now. As well intentioned as the new seekers will be, they keep thinking the Avalonians came from near where you will live. As time goes on, the Avalonians can feel their energy and memories being pulled away towards Meare; all because of a clever political fabrication. That is why they are in the Marches now; stuck between two localities. Pulled one way by their birth place, and in another by their willingness to help the seekers, who, through no fault of their own have the wrong location."

He paused, and looked like he was trying to remember something, his voice went quiet, and he spoke,

"'The Keys to Avalon'

Over river Deva,

Thru Devana toon,

Seek Westiners door;

I' thee Holi Cruses Wall.

By the Vails of Wails,

May Avalon be found."

"I can see two missing lines from the beginning."

"They are not lines perse that you see; for they are the two keys," said Pan.

"Above, the land of fathers."

"Within, the mothers womb."

*

In chapter 5, On their arrival in Meare, Lutrin and Malceni heard Uriel telling one of his ancient Finni stories: "The Finni maidens gathered up his poor dead body and prepared Gilwain for his burial. The fingertips that had fought Astaroth now lay still. Hands that had shown love to his people just hung by his side. The sparkling eyes that had enchanted Lalila only glared up at them like a kala on dry land. His golden hair, soft and fine as a new baby, was now matted with his own congealed blood. His heart, one that only desired tranquility for all, now lay unbeating on the ground. Life's blood had all but drained away, together with the greatest Halffinni that the world had ever known." Uriel paused, "And here endeth part one of the 'Lay of Gilwain' as was written in 'Lucid', a 'Book of light'." *

In chapter 12, after meeting Umov, Malceni had the following message for him:

MITHRAISM

Before Umov returned to Orcades, Malceni called him to one side. "Are you determined to revive the Persian structure of Mithraism and the bull cult; the world's first known and recorded religion?"

"How did you know where we first came from?"

"There is a little story that I would like to show you." Malceni pulled out his mirror and read the text to Umov,

"And so it was that the Persian beliefs of Mithraism were revived, incorporating the story of the fall from heaven of a disgraced brother, the flood, the Virgin birth of Mithras, the worship of him and the sharing of bread and wine on a Sunday, Mithras' day. The highlight of the year was his birthday on the 25th December. Mithras was crucified and laid to rest in a cave. He then came back to life and celebrated the Last Supper*.

It was a peaceful structure until those from the 'seven hills' heard that it was the beliefs of warriors; they thought that Mithras must be a warrior god. In time, blood thirsty rituals were introduced and the name of Mithras became a battle cry. Women became excluded from their rituals.

Many more years passed and a wise and wonderful man was born in the East. When he died, his followers formed a peaceful community based on love and equality for all. This community, for reasons unknown, incorporated many of the ancient Mithras rituals and myths.

* All of the above Mithraic beliefs predate both Judaism and Christianity.

For hundreds of years the two organisations were in competition for followers and then suddenly, overnight, Mithraism disappeared. But that was, in fact, an illusion.

Mithraism had covertly taken over its rival. As such, women were excluded from their rituals and the ideas of a 'Just War' became acceptable - in spite of the fact that the man born in the East was non-violent; as was Mithraism originally. It is still ruled from the 'seven hills'..."

Malceni stopped reading. "Will you still revive Mithraism?"

Umov was unmoved. "That may well be the story of this time-line, but a man must live for today and do what he thinks is right. Hear me Malceni, without a structure of belief Orcades will descend into chaos. The Orci may even turn to Thoth again if times get rough. I have to fill the space with something. The people must have their illusions and those illusions must be fed. For example, take away the illusion of life and all you have is the illusion of death. Which one would you choose?"

Lutrin, having overheard their conversation, walked over and appeared before them. "I prefer to create my own illusions and not to be tied to someone else's."

*

Pan knew about the Mithraism. He could have told them that it was quite natural what was going to happen. 'Even if it looks good, then because it is false it will eventually become bad in order to maintain the balance.'

**

In chapter 12, on the night of the bondings, Tilli had the following tale to tell:

Tilli's story about the wolf.

Tilli was surrounded by human children all demanding that he tell them the story he'd promised earlier. "What type of story would you like to hear?" he asked.

"Tell us one about a nasty wolf that eats people!" shouted one.

"No. I want to hear the story of Oliver Nogg in 'The Toggle Sprite'," said another.

"Okay, make yourselves comfortable. I do not know of this Toggle story, so it will have to be one with a wolf in it. This is the true story of Beddgelert, as told by Gridolers and not humans. It is a favourite of the young Griduini.

Diggle was not a very good carer, for one day he went out and left his baby in a cot, all alone. In the house was his best friend, Beddgelert the hound. 'I wonder what baby tastes like?' thought the hound, as he nibbled the baby's little toe. The baby started to cry of course; you would too if someone bit your little toe. 'A baby crying,' thought Karnak the Wolf, who was just outside the front door, 'I'd better see if I can help'.

When Karnak entered the house and saw what the hound was doing he rushed over and started a fight in order to rescue the baby. A fight to the death. Beddgelert was bigger than Karnak and, sadly, killed him.

During the struggle, the cot was knocked over on top of Karnak's body, and the baby went a-rolling under Diggle's bed. The hound was too big to get under the bed. The baby, now safe, fell asleep.

When Diggle finally came home, he saw blood on Beddgelert's lips and no sign of the baby. He was furious with the dog and cut off its head with his sword. Of course, after he'd done this he heard the baby crying under the bed. He picked the baby up and went to straighten out the cot. He was shocked to discover the dead wolf on the floor.

'My poor Beddgelert,' he said, 'what have I done?' Of course, not being very bright, Diggle thought that his hound had saved the baby. From that day onwards humans became scared of wolves and gave them a bad time".

"That's not how I heard it!" shouted one.

"Me neither!" agreed another.

"Let's go and see Tove. He always has a good yarn," said the first.

"Sorry," said Tilli, "must be off to sing a song."

Lutrin started giggling. "There was no way Tilli was going to say anything horrible about a wolf."

*

At the end of chapter 13, Malceni handed Lutrin a copy of what he had written about a horrible dream he had.

'Malceni's nightmare'

Although Lutrin was aware that Malceni was still in pursuit, he also knew that Amergin would want to know what he now saw. Peering a thousand feet over the cliff's edge, above Tyne-Cave point, he noticed the Dogger people were desperately trying to keep their little floaters from sinking beneath the waves. Their stubborn refusal to heed the warning signs given by the rising tide had resulted in the loss of many lives. Bodies, already bereft of life were being pounded against the rock face. Some of the people approaching the cliff tried in vain to climb up, only to be swept up, taken back and then flung by a merciless sea upon the rocks. Lutrin couldn't let them die. He had to show them the hidden cave that led under the Tajem forest. Their sun was starting to descend in the bright-night sky. Time to consider his actions was not an option, but as he made to stand up he felt a foot push his face to the ground.

'I was going to tip you over, but the mirror might break. Give it to me.'

'You have been deceived Malceni; both you and I have been used. They appealed to your greed and to my desire for change. I must tell you about ...'

'Too late, too late,' howled Malceni in despair. 'I'm irreparably damaged! Ruined! Down there, I'll be like them.'

"No," Lutrin soothed gently, "It is but a temporary ailment. Come back with me before this story makes Urs of us all. We will go together. Friends again, you and I."

The madness in Malceni's aura began to fade.

'Yes?' projected Lutrin.

'Yes,' whimpered Malceni.

'See, your tura understands me.' Lutrin held out his hand, only to see Malceni sliding towards the cliff edge and the madness reappear. The look in those eyes, as they disappeared into the night, held a mixture of hurt, fear and betrayal. Malceni was gone; falling without a sound into the chasm below.

Lutrin looked down in horror and turned away to see Taesus standing before him. "There was nothing you could do," he said solemnly. "Don't blame yourself."

The two gazed back to where Malceni had fallen, pain filling their hearts and minds. A glimmer of light from beneath them attracted their attention. "My people. You must help them."

"I was about to earlier," replied Lutrin.

As they made haste to the secret entrance of the cave, they heard voices. Realisation passed between them that the Dogger people had discovered the route.

'Impossible,' thought Lutrin, 'unless .... .'

"Shhh. Listen."

Within the darkness Fecir's voice could be heard, "One good turn my little friend deserves another. You shall have your revenge, but don't complain when you get it."

Appendix 2

The 'MISSING' song

As was the case for the missing stories, in order to keep the story flowing, the following song was removed.

In chapter 4, Garaldina sang **'Lament for a sister'** *for Lutrin:*

Swift as the wind breeze.

Loyal as the Moonrise.

As lovely as the Sun, and as

Pale as the snow.

On Panara, princess nara

My Panara, nara nara

So kind to me,

Her love to all.

She put me back,

Upon the right track,

When e'r I strayed,

In my youthful days.

On Panara, princess nara,

My Panara, nara nara

But now you've gone,

Where none can follow.

No magic light,

Or the turas sight,

Will bring you home,

This dreadful night.

Oh Panara, princess nara

My Panara, nara nara

Oh Panara, My Panara

Language

The poetic verses throughout the story were written with an
iambic rhythm; but some do reflect a more ancient meter of
composition, where the most important 'words of meaning'
are at the beginning and the end of each line.   Alas; the
'Babel' language, which used many words from many
cultures, no longer exists.   What little we have left can only
be read in the 'Books of Light'; and they are very hard to
find today.   As an example of its richness, here is the
original Babel version of the 'The Keys to Avalon'.   Apart
from the title and the two keys, the iambic is coincidentally
sustained in the ancient style also.

*

Den ties ut Avalon:

Uber flumen Deva,

Rastas Devana toon,

Soge Westiners borth;

I' Holi Cruses Wand.

Per Vails chan Lamentor,

Darf Avalon bod seydla.

Edella, terra chan Abbas,

Dentro, les Matris womb.

*

Appendix 4 (Chapter 14: 'A new beginning')

'The alternative ending'

Many years later, the Roc was still enjoying the taste of the various types of food that she could catch over the channel, but her back and stomach had been bothering her for some time. Today it was much worse, so she flew back to her nest for a rest. She had only recently enlarged the nest, which now took up a whole mountain plateau.

The pain was excruciating. 'After all my adventures,' she thought, 'to come to this.' Her sides started to contract, she stood up and, as she did so, an enormous egg dropped out. If she had not been the last Roc, another Roc could have told her that this was perfectly natural. Perplexed as she was, she was delighted that the pain had stopped. Instinctively, she wanted to keep the egg warm, which wasn't a problem in the hot climate that she lived in. And so, the last Roc set about ensuring that she wouldn't actually be the last Roc.

*

Tibias was on the move again. He made his way up the slopes of AnTara and, lighting a fire next to some large stones, poured a single drop of salty water onto each one. "That should be just enough," he said, and disappeared into the night.

The stones started to shimmer and take form in the moonlight. The first to reawaken was Bodgirn, ultimate guardian of the Firbolgs. They had no idea how long it had been since they had been chased out of Portowest. Fouglin, his snuggler, stood by his side. There was no sign of their daughter Linealay. Bouglin came over to them and, still feeling a bit stiff, bowed his head slowly.

"Well?" asked Bodgirn.

Bouglin shook his head. "She was last seen falling into the sea."

They all knew that even if she had 'become as stone' the salt water would eventually have eaten into her. Bodgirn wanted revenge.

Firbolgs were very similar to Picts in their bodily form. Not having a tura, they were also a little jealous of the Picts and claimed that they had left them because of it. The truth however, was that the Picts could not accept the Firbolgs wild emotional tempers anymore because it attacked their turas and caused them considerable head pains.

Not having a tura, Fouglin ignored her 'feeling' – the feeling that Linealay was still alive – because surely she could not still be alive after all this time. 'I do not have a tura,' she thought, 'so this is nonsense'.   Bouglin was having strange feelings too. Whilst he had been 'sleeping' all those years, he had dreams that he had seeded a son. 'I am turaless,' he thought, 'so why can I hear Linealay's pain'. Fouglin and Bouglin turned and stared at each other. 'We can hear feelings. Not just words'.

*

In truth, Fecir had seeded another son. A warrior by all accounts. Now in his teens, some say he was born standing up and had fought his way out of the womb. Born with only one eye, they called him Sullibhan; the one-eyed man. His brother Taesus, who now lived happily in Orcades, gave Sulli a present from a far off land. It was a one-eyed Monkey!

*

The Woodwose, still looking very happy with his oak-life, had informed Pan that when the three wizards had arrived, all those years ago, one of the Finns was the harbour master that day and not a human. As such, Aniel's tree fragment might not have gone to the right wizard.

"I asked Amergin to give it to the harbour master because it was quite likely that he couldn't see me. I do not make mistakes," said Pan, "my nature does not permit it. Amergin was the one who talked about a human. In the long-term he is right, but I'm not discussing this now," he concluded, somewhat impatiently.

Shortly after Pan had visited the Woodwose, he felt a tingling in his horns. Something required his attention. 'Time I introduced myself to a wizard,' he thought, 'adventures aren't much fun alone. Now, who can I take with me?'

*

In the Caledonius Saltus mountains, things weren't looking good. In years past, the Orci had killed many of the wild animals, and now Picts had come to live in the region. The real problem was that there was now a lack of food in the troll-nests of the Lugi. Nobody had heard of, or even seen a 'troll'. Naturally shy creatures, they had been happy with this situation in the past; but not anymore.

*

Aniel had been plagued with doubt. He didn't truly know if he was forgiven or not. He decided that there was only one way to find out. 'I need a ship,' he thought.

*

Meanwhile, Malceni had left a letter, from Tilli in Castletown, lying on his favourite chair by the fire. He had just left the house to go and tell Lutrin about it when Margaret, now sixteen, picked up the letter. She only had time to read, .'.. and about this Dragon,' and 'PS: I finally learnt to speak wolf,' when she heard Titch calling her name.

As he stepped into the sunlight, Malceni stopped briefly. He saw a face on his tura. A face which, although he did not know why, he was sure that he recognised.

*

Around this time, Lutrin, now aged forty-three, called nineteen year old Tibboha into his reading room and brought out the Roc whistle. Tibboha came in munching. He was worried that his father may have discovered his secret ability, an ability that Tibboha didn't know was passed down to him from his soul-mother.

"If you are in real need of help. I mean, if you find yourself in a life threatening situation," said Lutrin, "and none are around to help you, use this."

"What is it for?"

"Sit down Tibbs. I have a very long story to tell you."

*

The end?

A voice cried out, 'The Picts will return!'
And the people said, 'Who is this?'

The voice cried again, 'The Faeries will return!'
And the people said, 'What is this?'

Then Lucid did write, 'Here, read the truth.'
And the people said, 'The Picts have returned!'

Then Pan did say, 'Here, see the truth!'
And the people all cried,
'The Faeries, the Faeries have returned!'

*

Author biography / background to the work.

After obtaining a Theology degree from Liverpool University, Mark Youds embarked on a science career before training to become a Religious Education teacher. He has several granted Patents and two University (Dundee and Bristol) published science papers. At the age of forty-five however, Mark fulfilled his desire to write a dialectic Anglo-Irish myth tinged with a little new age philosophy that espouses individual spirituality, rather than a structure of belief.

'A Pictish Tale: Bryhery Gap' is a pseudo-historical fantasy that would sit comfortably alongside the works of Paulo Coelho and Richard Bach; in contrast to a philosophy though, it is the drama and inter-relationship of the characters which is emphasised in the text.

Although the setting is eight thousand years ago, the central characters could collectively be likened to an enlightened 21st century 'Everyman' – as they grapple with a world where the ego, the sub-conscious and the differences between a soul and a spirit are critical to survival.

Mark has one grown-up daughter, and lives with his wife in County Kerry, Eire.

*

www.ingramcontent.com/pod-product-compliance
Lightning Source LLC
Chambersburg PA
CBHW031107260626
47172CB00001B/265